THORA

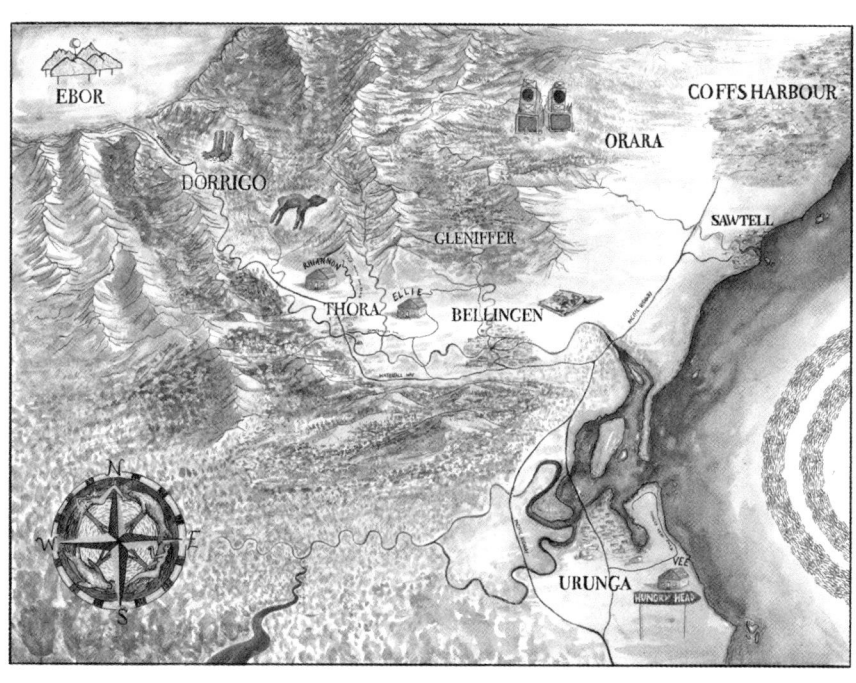

WORMS PUBLISHING

© 2024 Tilly Lawless

Published in Australia in February 2024
Published in the UK in June 2024

All rights reserved. No part of this book may be reproduced or transmitted in any form or by any means, electronic or mechanical, including photocopying, recording or by any information storage and retrieval system, without prior permission in writing from the publisher.

Worms Limited
32 Sackville Street
W1S 3EA
United Kingdom
Email: studio@worm-s.com
Web: www.wormsmagazine.com

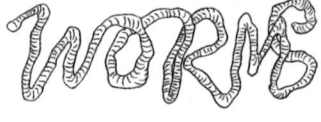

Cover Illustration and Sleeve: Rufus Shakespeare
Editor: Clem MacLeod
Assistant Editors: Caitlin McLoughlin, Arcadia Molinas
Assistant Sub-editor: Enya Sullivan
Manuscript Editor: Elena Gomez
Orkney Dialect Editor: Leah Moodie

Typesetting by: Caitlin McLoughlin

ISBN 978-1-3999-7341-0

Printed in China

THORA

TILLY LAWLESS

To country girls, girls with difficult relationships with their mothers and any girl who has been called 'off the rails.'

1

2009 was drawing to a close and Rhiannon was bringing it to a very insalubrious end by getting expelled from her local public high school. Her mother was furious, having to fork out for a private school fifty kilometres away, and her friends were devastated. For Rhiannon, though, the worst part was that she was going to have to wake up half an hour earlier in the mornings, and half an hour at sixteen was an eternity. Her body needed the sleep; she was a teenager for god's sake! Every minute of sleep she lost was ten brain cells in her mind or one grade percentile or a lost job opportunity in her twenties, or so she was told. Not that she cared about that. What it actually meant was one less half hour she could spend on the family computer at night, holed up in the computer room having sex with strangers on Omegle, with the door wide open so that her mother wouldn't find it suspicious and come barging in, hunched over the screen with fingers inside her pyjama shorts and a sly eye on the door, 'ASL?' the only foreplay.

Her laptop was useless for these late-night endeavours, it didn't have internet, it was just a companion to watch movies with, feeding films into its slit as the flying foxes feasted on the fig tree outside her window, low hanging branches brushing against the glass. The same fig that she had nestled a baby tawny frogmouth into when she found him fallen on the ground, all grumpy brows and feathered toes and glum beak that swallowed whole the chunks of raw steak she surreptitiously cut from their groceries, keeping him private as she instinctively did all things. She wanted to fold in on herself, crept around the house on tiptoe, felt like Chuchundra in *Rikki-Tikki-Tavi*, pressed against the walls and hoped to become a part of them, to live her life unnoticed. Instead her mother forced confidences with prying fingers and sharp accusations, and saved honeyed words for when Rhiannon's friends came round, charming them with a cleverness that was mistaken for kindness.

'Your mum's so nice!' was the phrase she heard the most, and never contradicted.

It hurt to hear, and it hurt even more to remember what it had been like when she was younger. Moments of physical intimacy – being read a book aloud, fiddling with the necklace around her mother's neck – replaced with emotional persecution as she aged. The smarter she got, the longer her legs grew, the more attention she commanded in a room, the more Angela viewed her as competition. Rhiannon had pared away at the relationship between them, just as she pared away at herself at night with scissors in hand, and she knew that her mother was only acting out the same dynamic with her that she'd had with her own mother, a working-class woman who had chomped at the fetters binding her, had wanted to study but ended up working the floor of David Jones for forty years. Rhiannon's grandmother had resented her daughter's intelligence, an intelligence that was allowed to achieve more in the eighties than she had been able to in the fifties. Angela was both shaped and bound by the feminist theory of the second wave, as well as scarred and made paranoid by her ex-husband's constant infidelity with younger women. Like her mother before her who resented an educated woman, Angela hated any overtly sexual or feminine women, and as Rhiannon 'bloomed,' as Proust would say, their relationship grew all the more fractious.

People tried to tell her that it was natural not to get along with your mother at that age, and she had overheard Angela's friends consoling her with the same. Wasn't teenagerhood just one long assertion of personhood, an untangling from the womb, a defiant foot stamp echoing in every slammed door and secret sip of liquor, a declaration of separateness and despair at knowing that you were birthed into the world with a mark upon you? Not a tabula rasa as you might wish, but carrying your parents along with you in the way you spoke and the way you set a table and if you kissed people hello or not. You saw that umbilical cord with every step, and god it shackled you like a chain.

Rhiannon dreamed of being an orphan, like protagonists in books, not for the squalor but for the freedom of coming from *nothing*. Who would she be without her mum to trip up her life? Not realising that that was the real her, right there, intrinsically tied up with her and not any more compromised by the having of a parent than an orphan is compromised by the not having. They both shape you. Just as her grandmother had shaped her mother before her and would still call and harass Angela over the phone, and then ask to speak to her granddaughter and coo to her, not realising that that bitterness had to be displaced somewhere, and was going to land on her beloved granddaughter.

It was the last day before term four started, and a heat haze smudged the casuarinas along the river. The tar road melted to Rhiannon's feet as she walked to join her best friend, Ellie. She lived six kilometres away, in the next interlocking valley, but they had arranged to meet for a morning swim at a quiet bridge halfway between them. She set out barefoot, skin soft and sensitive from a winter spent in shoes; it was time to toughen them up for the long summer ahead. The bitumen was sticky and malleable beneath the sun, as glaring a sun as if it were high summer and not October. If she were younger she would've played with it in her hands, now she just let it stain her soles symbolically for the season, in the same way mulberry stains may mark the beginning of spring.

When she had awoken that morning she had gotten out of bed immediately, loath to stay when the sheets clung to her with sweat. It was going to be one of those days where the thermometer on the back porch hit thirty degrees by 9am. She'd sweltered and suffocated all night, but if she opened the windows for the night breeze she was tormented by mozzies, or a lone bat flitting desperately above her head, trying to escape again. One year she had given up and let the bats roost in her room during the heat of the day, feeling like a vampire queen as they flew out each twilight from her window, hosting her quick-winged creatures in her own bed chamber. Till her mum found out and made her shut them out, grumbling about Hendra virus and possible parasites. If she wanted undisturbed sleep it was always better to keep the windows firmly closed, and have only her sweat as a consort.

She had paused on the verandah as she brushed her hair, watching the letter-winged kites that nested each year at the top of the hoop pine circle, relishing the time alone with the valley before Angela awoke. She tried to count the flame trees, splashes of red burst into flower on the mountain, and watched swallows flit round, circuiting the house again and again as they ate up all the bugs brought forth by the heat. The rough wood felt cool beneath her bare feet and she gazed at one of the poles holding up the porch; the knots in the wood looked silky smooth, textured so like a lemur's fur in oscillating waves and breaks. She liked to imagine the creatures were somehow trapped in there, living in the pine as their coats glistened in the sun, but when she put her skin up against it, it was always splinters of disappointment and no company. After she did her chores (letting out the chooks who cluttered past her and clucked in delight with outstretched-wings, and also checking the shared water trough of the cows and Tall, the Shetland pony) she set off with Ajax, the kelpie cross, trotting beside her.

The valleys around Bellingen were eclectic, communes of hippies next to secluded pianists, retired TV anchors and farming families that had been there for generations. Like most fertile places in Australia, ideal for the cultivation of stock and crops, the genocide committed by the white colonialists was all the more brutal. And while the places around carried Gumbaynggirr names, it was a mostly white area – and the names were possibly mispronounced anyway, the culture was so disrespected.

Ellie teased Rhiannon for coming from the smallest, most unknown valley – more backwards than Darkwood, more enigmatic than Kalang and without the trendiness of Gleniffer. It was true that Little North Arm was forgotten, a dead-end road that snaked off Waterfall Way just before it began to climb up the mountain, through the Gondwana rainforests and on to the farming land at the top. Her neighbours consisted of an old salt-of-the-earth cattle farmer, who condescended to advise them on their own measly herd of two, an heiress who wanted a rainforest retreat and a family man who sneaked off from his wife and passel of kids whenever it was evening feed time to mastubrate along their adjoining fence line while Rhiannon fed Tall. She hadn't told anyone about this, it made her far too uncomfortable to even think of explaining it, but it was disconcerting having a naked man with a hard-on prowl up and down the fence line, separated from her by only a few metres and some strands of barbed wire. One time Ellie came along with her and he was there again, shamelessly stroking himself as they both averted their eyes.

'That was weird,' Rhiannon said, almost apologetically and as if it didn't always happen, and they never spoke about it again.

It was early enough in the morning that even by the time Rhiannon got to Summervilles Road and found Ellie already waiting and swinging her legs over the side of the wooden bridge, the waterhole was empty. It wasn't one of the more well known ones that tourists frequented anyway. It wasn't deep enough and it didn't have a rope swing or space to camp. It was mainly used by local kids who couldn't yet drive, or parents with small children, being the perfect depth for paddling – the water only went above your head once you swam under the bridge itself. Still, Rhiannon loved it. It was beautiful and it was hers and Ellie's, where they had spent countless summer days swatting March flies away while sucking mangoes in the shallows, and where they had met the local boys and bartered for cans of Bundy over a makeshift fire on the rocks at night. After it flooded, the river was still high enough that it swept you over constellations of rocks that you would usually have to rock hop through, they could start with boogie boards at Rhiannon's and ride it 3km down to the little bridge, exhilarated and with bruised shins from each conglomeration they couldn't quite clear.

'You going to drink *Jesus Juice* now?' Ellie mocked her, snide with a barely-disguised jealousy.

'I don't even know what that means. Isn't that what Catholics do? I think this is Anglican.'

'You'll get back so late now that we won't be able to go here together after school,' Ellie moodily threw rocks not suitable for skipping into the water.

'I know it sucks. Let's not talk about it, it makes me too devo.'

They spent an hour swimming beneath the bridge, holding on to the planks and being shaken by the vibrations as cars went overhead, grabbing each other's ankles from below and clutching at each other's waists. Gradually more people came down and shattered their solitude, and as it reached lunchtime hunger knocked at their stomachs.

'Do you wanna come back to mine and eat lunch and punch some billies? I'm fiending it,' Ellie asked.

Rhiannon quickly agreed and they began to walk towards Ellie's house, where she also lived alone with her single mum. Ellie was half Burmese, raised by her white mother, and in such a rural area she stood out. She was known as a 'hasian' at school – a portmanteau for 'hot Asian.' Her home was a haven to Rhiannon; Sasha seemed to her to be Angela's polar opposite. She wondered if she would've let her keep feeding the three baby rats nesting in her cupboard, deserted by their mother (who had probably fallen victim to the cruel rat poison beneath the sink), instead of unceremoniously turning them out, with the rags they had nursed in thrown in the bin.

They ran themselves under the garden hose when they got back, already dried out from their walk, and left wet footprints all the way to Ellie's bedroom. Over a cone of mostly stems, a pitiful ransack from Ellie's mum's stash, Ellie declared, 'Well, I guess this is farewell to 2454.'

'Hey, I'm not leaving Thora! I'm only going to school in Coffs. It's not like I'll be from there.'

'Yeah but you'll probably start hanging with all the Coffs boys and girls and won't come to Tallowwood Point or Brownlee's Lane anymore.'

There was a pause before Rhiannon could answer, as the Gatorade bong bubbled and she pulled, held it in as long as her lungs could bear and let it out with a painful cough.

'Na, if I do go to anything new I'll invite you too, obviously.' She put the bong down carefully next to the bed and failed at waving the smoke out the window before adding, 'and besides, it's only for a term. After that we can both go to CHEC for year eleven.'

'Should we watch something?' Ellie squatted down on the floor and perused a pile of DVDs as her wet hair dripped onto the carpet.

'Yeah, you got anything new from the video store?'

'Na coz I've got late fines, I have to pay those off if I wanna rent anything, so annoying.'

'Pass me what you've got, I'm too baked to move right now,' Rhiannon flicked through. 'Let's just watch *Finding Nemo*. The colours are so pretty.' They were well into the father fish's journey, squid careening through the ocean currents, when a voice broke into their reverie.

'You girls stoned again?' It was Sasha, signature smoke in hand. Late thirties with curly hair and perky tits, her irreverence made her seem ten years younger. Rhiannon had a crush of admiration on her, so deep she hadn't even admitted it to herself, let alone her friend.

'On such a nice day too, you should be outside enjoying it.' She punctuated this with an ash of her cigarette over Ellie's window ledge.

'Sashaaaa, we already went for a swim! Leave us alone.' Rhiannon could never get used to Ellie calling her mum by her first name, or the dynamic between them at all, and held herself more formally than usual, largely incapacitated by awe over the way they interacted. The pretend disregard and real mutual tenderness so apparent between them was both alien and wonderful, and couldn't be disturbed in case it disintegrated.

'Okay it's your last day of holidays so you can do what you want, just remember no smoking on school nights. Rhi, Ellie tells me you've been expelled?'

'Asked to leave, that's what I said!' Ellie leapt to her own and Rhiannon's defence.

'Same thing, just a euphemism. Anyway I thought you'd be proud to claim that. Doesn't it add a notch to your belt, a bit of street cred? It used to when I was your age.'

Rhiannon, withered before her direct gaze and acerbic wit, finally managed to summon up an answer through her stoned haze and burped a pathetic 'Yeah, I guess.'

'Well, I hope you like the new school. Ellie will certainly miss not having you around as much. Now, both of you take off your wet bikinis before you end up with thrush.' And with that, she was gone, and the room was as it was before.

Sasha neutralised rebellion by making it seem like the most mundane conformity because she had done it all before. Ellie couldn't take up smoking, couldn't cough an illicit cough beneath her doona cover, because her mum had beaten her to it and would just say, as she stubbed out her smoke, 'It's nice to see some things stay the same; kids still want to ruin their lungs. Makes me feel young again.' She couldn't sneak out at night to meet Rhiannon, the night alive with crickets and cows' mournful eyes spooking her through bunches of Parramatta grass, because her mum would say, 'If you decide to take a spontaneous night time ramble again make sure you don't sleep through your alarm.' She couldn't even watch forbidden movies – at twelve years old, when she first saw *Fight Club*, her mum picked up the DVD case and said, 'good movie,' before sauntering off, cigarette held aloft, mighty and undefeated. She invited confidences through her nonchalance, was adored by all the girls and ostracised by the other parents as a threat to order. With the tunnel vision of youth, Ellie never wondered what her mum, an intelligent woman who soaked up culture like she did smoke, thrived off conversation and had travelled widely alone in her teens, was doing tucked away beneath the Great Dividing Range, fifteen kilometres out of a tiny town, isolated and working as – what exactly? – at some sort of office job. She never wondered what mistakes in her own upbringing Sasha was trying not to repeat in her daughter's, or what world she was keeping her from.

Sasha, sorting through condoms behind a closed bedroom door, was glad her daughter had no curiosity about her, no inkling of her work. For the thousandth time she sorted through the mess of her mind, debating whether or not she should tell her daughter. And for the thousandth time decided 'not yet.'

2

In her new uniform, a starched shirt with a tie and blazer, Rhiannon felt like she was in class drag. She was going to be with all the rich kids – did this make her a rich kid? It wasn't like her lifestyle was going to change, though. She'd still had to get on two rickety country buses, with torn vinyl seats, windows that jammed and metal poles that burned you in both heat and cold. The final bus was an airconditioned one, that now sped along the freeway, exporting all these kids from the valley to the supposedly superior schooling of Coffs Harbour, depositing them out the front of a school you had to pay for, and that made you go to chapel.

Coffs Harbour was once a feared target of the Japanese in World War II because it had an airport, a train station and a sea port. Now, due to its strategic position on the Pacific Highway exactly halfway between Brisbane and Sydney, it was simply a hub for trucks and drug flow between states. Coffs Harbour, full of surfers, tacky motels and homophobia. The catchment for her new school spread as far inland as Ebor, one hundred kilometres away, stretched as far south as Macksville and as far north as Corindi. Rhiannon was disheartened by this distance; it was already hard enough to hang out with her old school friends when they lived in scattered valleys around the town, always having to scab a lift somehow because there were no trains and no buses on the weekend. Now whoever she befriended could live more than an hour away – what was the point in even making new friends?

She sighed and shrugged down into herself and the bus seat simultaneously, contemplating hiding on the bus till it did the round trip all the way back to Bello back to Bello – where she would talk her friends into skipping class to spend the day by the river. They would surely be on to her missing the very first day though and she would get home from a peaceful day to have her mother on her back... it wasn't worth it. She would have to push through. She tried to scope out the age of the people on her bus, as at least then they would come from a similar area to her.

But the only ones who looked around her age were sitting near the front, and she was too intimidated to approach anyone older or further back than her. School buses always had an obvious hierarchy, ranked by age and social status, with the coolest sitting at the back.

The bus left the highway and began hurtling along windy dirt roads, the driver confidently taking the turns with a spray of gravel. Rhiannon tried to imagine the ferns weren't grey with dust, but spangled with silver like the magic valley of *The Little White Horse*. She could still disappear into the imaginary when need be, and with each paddock that appeared in a cutaway slice between blurred sped-by forest she pictured herself galloping along on the little white horse, keeping up with the school bus but visible to no one.

At the last stop before the bus returned to the highway, the final person to get on was a girl who looked about the same age as her, given she was dressed in the 'senior' uniform. Rhiannon watched her with a degree of interest she hadn't watched anyone else with, noting details that her eyes had simply passed over with the others. The girl's skirt was hiked up higher than the uniform restrictions allowed, she had a frayed leather thong tied around her slender wrist, damp dark hair falling out of a loose bun, and one earphone in, while the other hung insouciantly on her shoulder. She leaked coolness just as her hair leaked water, a widening wet patch spreading on the back of her shirt. Rhiannon kept watching, entranced, as the girl sat in the first available seat, speaking to no one.

Rhiannon wanted to talk to her, be friends with her. So much so that when the bus pulled into her new school gates, she looked less at the school and more at the girl, trying to make fleeting eye contact and hoping the girl would say 'hey, you're new!' She didn't seem the type to do that, but still. As Rhiannon walked into the school grounds technicolour scenarios played out in her mind, of the girl in the classroom, having to take the only spare seat next to her. Of her getting her bag caught in Rhiannon's as they walked along a narrow corridor, of having to disentangle from each other and maybe briefly touch hands.

Rhiannon had her bag on a bench between two big swarming groups. One group of chattering girls, whose straightened hair and glinting lip glosses and proximity to some lounging surfer boys proclaimed them as the 'cool group,' and another group, slightly smaller and less loud and more gender mixed. As she scrounged around for her books for first period, a fat girl with dyed black hair and multiple facial piercings from the latter group gestured to her to move her bag closer.

'Hey, you can put your bag with us. I'm Zoe by the way. And this is Keira.' A strikingly tall and beautiful girl with brown skin gave a casual 'hey' from beside her before turning back to her own bag. She was Aboriginal, and Rhiannon quickly gathered that maybe she was with the girls who were ostracised from the coolest echelons of the schoolyard, for varying reasons.

'Thanks, I don't know anyone here. I'm Rhiannon.'

'Yeah I can tell. Who have you got for first period English? You might be with us if you're lucky.'

She was, and as they headed through the corridors together Zoe quizzed her on where she came from.

'Bellingen, hey? Yeah you won't fit in with them. They're all from that chain of beaches. Korora, Sapphire, maybe even Korora Basin if their house is big enough. I mean, don't get me wrong, you're pretty enough. The guys'll love you just like they love Keira.'

But Rhiannon didn't care about the guys loving her. She just wanted the girls to. And to know about the girl from her bus that morning. She described her to them both, haltingly and nervous without understanding why. Though she felt drawn to girls in a way she never did to guys, and she had admitted to Ellie after a read of the sealed section in *Dolly* mag that she was 'bicurious but like definitely don't ever want to go there I'm just, like, curious about people who are gay and stuff you know,' she had not recognised her fascination as attraction.

Zoe wondered aloud as to who it could be before Keira said, 'She's talking about Vanora.' She turned to Rhiannon and added, 'she's in our maths class.'

'Ohhh, Vanora! Oh yeah, she's cool. But she's a massive ice queen. You won't ever get to know her. She keeps to herself. Except supposedly she's a bit of a slut, though I've never even seen her talk to a guy but outside school apparently it's a different story.'

'She's a strange one. She doesn't fit.' Keira looked at Rhiannon directly when she said this, almost as if warning her. But it meant nothing to Rhiannon. Her mind was echoing with Vanora's name, as the V crashed against her cranium and the softness of the rest rolled and washed and darted within. Vanora. A name to write a poem about, to sing an ode to, to hang a badge on. A name to fold up into a little note and carry in your pocket, to mull over and trace the letters of.

Her mind snagged on the second statement, a harsh condemnation in high school, where all everyone wanted was to not stand out, to shave off their square peg sides and be one among many. What did Keira mean, she didn't fit? How could a pretty, skinny white girl not fit in a coastal high school? And for Keira to say this, the only one whose ancestors hadn't come in boat loads of immigrants, or planes fleeing from far off war, whose ancestors had been there for millennia and now was vilified as if it were *her* that didn't belong.

'What do you mean she doesn't fit?'

But now they were entering the classroom and her question went unanswered.

Rhiannon's first day passed in a blur, the only memorable part was the hour she spent in the same room as Vanora for a year ten assembly, unable to muster up the courage to smile at her let alone speak to her, but hyperconscious of the fact that they breathed the same air, that the same oxygen tickled both their lungs and the same school bell assaulted both their ears. She watched her fiddle with the leather thong around her wrist and wondered if her hands were calloused, wondered if the lines she drew across her knuckles in biro had any meaning or were simply the scratches of an overactive mind, till the teacher noticed her distraction and told her off in front of the year for daydreaming.

At recess and lunch, she was grateful to join Zoe and Keira, not condemned to eat alone as the new kid. Their friend Cam joined them too, a sardonic boy with a side fringe that he had to keep sweeping out of his eyes. He caught the bus into school with Keira, as they both came from out Orara way, though he seemed to hate the area, dismissing it as a 'boil on the butt of Cowper.'

'It's actually beautiful,' Keira said defensively. 'His home is one of the nicest places in Karangi, he just hates it coz he hates cows.'

'Hates cows?'

'It's a cattle farm. Angus.' He flicked his wrist witheringly. How someone could hate cows Rhiannon had no idea, but she could see he had dreams beyond a Karangi beef cattle farm, no matter how beautiful.

'Are you out that way too, Zoe?'

'Na, I'm at –'

'19 O!' interjected Cam, before she could finish.

Keira snorted and Zoe rolled her eyes, Rhiannon looked confused. 'That's such a tired joke Cam, and she wouldn't get it anyway. 19 Orlando Street is the Coffs brothel. He's just saying that coz I live in Park Beach right near it.'

'Oh wow, there's a brothel in Coffs? Do you like, see the women walking out of it? What do they look like?'

'The prostitutes you mean? They're pretty underwhelming like, they're always in tracksuits and carrying a big bag. Sometimes they're even in slippers. One wears pink mini skirts and hectic heavy make-up though, and has huge fake tits. She's Cam's favourite. He always keeps an eye out for her when he stays at mine, don't ya?'

'I even got to speak to her once,' Cam said to Rhiannon, sotto voce. 'She was waiting at the same bus stop as me and she asked if her lip liner was smudged and I said –'

'"No, you look incredible – I'm not saying you have drag queen makeup but a drag queen would *love* your makeup,"' interrupted Zoe.

'Hey, that's my line!'

'He tells that story so many times,' Zoe explained to Rhiannon. 'And besides I doubt you even really said it.'

'Poetic licence, babe. Just because you don't have an imaginative bone in your body, at least not one anyone could find under all that – '

'Can you two stop bickering for once? It's overwhelming,' Keira said. Zoe and Cam stopped, but the truce appeared tenuous.

'Hey guys,' Rhiannon asked. All three turned to look at her. 'I know you can be overwhelmed and underwhelmed, but can you ever just be whelmed?' They all relaxed into immediate laughter at the *10 Things I Hate About You* reference, and Keira smiled at her gratefully.

Rhiannon met her eyes with wry acknowledgement, and then looked beyond them, to where she could see a lone figure walking into the bushes surrounding the oval. With a rush of recognition she realised it was Vanora. What was she doing? They still had one period left. Was she sneaking off for a cone, to ease that final hour? Was she wagging it entirely? Or was she meeting a boy in those bushes? Was she about to get down on those fabled knees, take a teen cock into her notorious mouth, a cock that had the slight sour taste of urine because teen boys never wiped, always shook? Was he about to feel how warm and moist the inside of her cheeks were, was he going to send a sad squirt down the back of her throat so she gagged and spat it up in the wet leaves, was she going to come up with wet leaves on her knees too, that she would brush off with a quick hand so as not to give away her rendezvous? Was she going to catch the bus home afterwards, and bump those same knees against the seat in front, were they stubbled with regrowth or smooth or a soft down like Rhiannon's? Did she stuff them under her school jumper when she was sad, tuck her head inside and smell the vinegar waft from her pre-menstrual pussy? Was she comforted by the familiar scent of her cunt, like Rhiannon was? Did she hold her hand against it when she fell asleep? Did she hope to hold someone inside it too? But, most of all, had she noticed Rhiannon like she'd noticed her?

3

The first two weeks of term had passed, and Rhiannon was a little drunk and a lot stoned as she stumbled home along the gravel road on a late Sunday afternoon, heading back from Ellie's after having spent the weekend with her as always, nothing having changed in spite of Ellie's doom and gloom prediction. Night was falling and she sat down on the grass verge, bullrushes tickling her nostrils as she looked at the soles of her feet. She couldn't entirely make them out in the dusk, but they were definitely hurting, though dulled by the drugs, and there was definitely something that looked like a squashed pomegranate on the ball of both of them.

'Look at you,' she said to them blearily, inexplicably in an English accent. 'Where have you been? How did you two mix with pomegranates? Pom-mee-gran-ats,' she enunciated slowly; that word sounded good in a posh accent.

She had another four kilometres to walk home, which equalled four kilometres of gravel to cut up her bare feet, and four kilometres to sober up so that when she got home in time for dinner her mum wouldn't know. Her mum had never been a weed smoker thankfully, and so naively – or perhaps wilfully, in denial – accepted Rhiannon's smell as that of the hippy-incense irresponsible Sasha put on. Ellie and her had met at the bridge that morning, then decided they wanted to spend their Sunday drinking, so had walked back to Rhiannon's to fetch the goon sack she had hidden under a corner of the hen house. Passing it between them they took turns pretending to be pregnant, when it was held under their respective hoodies, as they walked back to Ellie's. Sasha was gone for the day – she sometimes did the odd Sunday shift at her office – and so they lolled about the house, pouring goon down each other's throats while the other one kneeled, missing more and more as they got progressively drunker, and flashed their tits on Chatroulette.

'Grass before beer you're in the clear, beer before grass you're on your arse,' Ellie sang, as Rhiannon fell over in the kitchen.

'Too late,' she said sheepishly, and the two laughed so much that Ellie ended up laying on the floor beside her.

Looking up at the ceiling Ellie reached across and grabbed Rhiannon's hand. They both fell quiet.

'Rhini, I'm so glad we still spend the weekends together.'

'Of course! You know I'd never ditch you. You're my BFF. I can't wait for us to be at CHEC together. Also, you're really gonna like the friends I've made at Bishop, and they're all gonna come too – Keira and Zoe and Cameron.'

'Is Cameron hot?'

'I mean, he is, but he's also like sooo gay.'

'Oh my god no way, do people know?'

'Na but like you can tell, for sure, it's obvious.' Rhiannon paused, and then asked, 'Imagine if I was like "I'm gay" right now. Jokes! But what would you be like?'

'Ummmm, I'd be like let go of my hand you creep! Na but seriously I'd be like, does she check me out?'

They had laughed till their sides hurt and Rhiannon remembered she needed to be home for dinner and cut the hilarity short. She couldn't ask her mum to pick her up because of the state she was in, not that she would've asked even if she were sober, knowing her mum would use the favour against her down the track. And unlike Ellie, who had her ex-racehorse mare Gemma to ride on, carrying her surely and safely even when she was inebriated, she wasn't a real horse girl who could ride home drunk. Her only option was to walk home, which is how she ended up traversing eighteen kilometres barefoot in one day, her feet bleeding well before she finally reached her house.

When Rhiannon finally made it through her front door, slightly sobered up from the long walk, she found her mother waiting for her at the dinner table already, presiding over it like a dark storm cloud, quivering with the torrent that Rhiannon sensed was about to gush forth. Before she could even sit down, her mother said, 'your father called earlier.'

'Oh okay, I'll call him back after dinner.'

Rhiannon's father who lived and worked interstate, had another family with two children and a wife. She didn't see him often but she got along with him, and was not traumatised by or resentful of his absence as people expected her to be. He had left when she was four and she couldn't even imagine living in close quarters with him or being close with him. But to her mother, it was like he had only left yesterday. She was still in active war with him, tried to turn Rhiannon into a mole, tried to ferret out facts from her.

'What is he working on these days?'

'I don't know I haven't –'

'And that woman? That Dutch woman. The Dutch are always such snobs. What's she doing?'

'I think maybe she's still –'

'And those children? I bet they don't get as good marks as you did. Your father was never smart, your brains come from my side.'

'Ummm I guess –'

'Not that you use yours enough. I know what you've been doing. I know that you've been sneaking out to see that boy down the road, sleeping with him for drugs. I don't know which friend you're getting them for – Ellie, or one of those new ones at that school with the exorbitant fees – but I know that's what you're doing. You can't pull the wool over my eyes.'

Rhiannon shovelled the salmon casserole into her mouth so that she could have an excuse not to acknowledge or answer the accusation, swallowing with barely a chew, ignoring the slight discomfort as some bones momentarily lodged in her throat. Her mind was frozen but the quicker she finished the meal the quicker she could leave the table, leave this bombardment. Where was this coming from? Which boy was she even talking about? She hadn't slept with any boys. Didn't even want to. Were these all things Angela had had said to her by someone else, was she unable to differentiate those rumours from the reality of the now, or herself from the image of her daughter?

'Nothing to say back, huh? What's wrong with you? Can't you express any emotions? Are you that emotionally crippled? Just eating away like your dumb father always did. Incapable of emotion.'

She knew she couldn't fight back. The times she had tried, her mum punished her for it. She'd refused to drop Rhiannon at the school bus in the morning so she missed school, and then got her in trouble all over again for that. She used to cut her pocket money too, the ten dollars a week gone, if she answered back, so she was trained into silence. Thankfully now she was sixteen the government support for low-income families went directly into her own bank account, so her mother couldn't confiscate that. But still, she had to endure!

'You can't trick me with this demureness, I know from those little shorts you wear that you're a slut. After all the boys. Promiscuous. Karen at the fish shop told me she saw you flirting with the chemist's son outside the post office the other day, the whole town knows what you're like so don't think you can pull the wool over *my* eyes. And now on top of that you're an emotional cripple! Can't even feel to react. What a combination.'

She was trying to bait her. Surely she couldn't mean those things, could she? Angela wanted a rise but for Rhiannon it was just a race to the finish, her mouth so close to the plate that her hair fell in the food, her eyes focused on nothing but the fork. Finally!

'Thank you for dinner. I'll wash up later. I just need to shower and finish this assignment first.' And she was off to the bathroom, knowing the mention of school work was the one thing Angela would respect, knowing there were razors waiting, knowing that she couldn't cry, so maybe she was emotionally crippled like her mum said, maybe there was something deeply wrong with her, deeper than the cuts she sliced on the tender inside of her upper arm.

'I feel sorry for you,' her mother called after her as Rhiannon placed her dish in the sink. 'You're going to have a very lonely life if you can't feel any emotions.'

The next day Rhiannon was moved up a maths class, to the one that Keira and Zoe were in. The school had been pleasantly surprised by her abilities, given she had been expelled from a public school and came with a slightly concerning record, having been in trouble for things like putting her whole tech class on to sex chat rooms and taking off her shirt in a science class. Even though she had insisted the latter was for a dare the school counsellor hadn't seen it that way, had seen it as a sign of promiscuity, of wanting to have the male teacher's sexual attention.

'Yuck! As if I'd ever want to sleep with Mr Hargrave!' Rhiannon had said to Ellie.

She sat on the middle row with Keira and Zoe, listened to the latest gossip about a girl in year eight who had sent a guy a photo of her sticking an Impulse deodorant can up her pussy only for him to print it out and sell it for $5 a shot at the hippy commune in Bundagen.

'Isn't that, like, child porn?' Keira asked.

'Yeah it's like pretty fucked,' Zoe agreed.

Rhiannon was no longer concentrating. Vanora had just walked in. How could she forget that she was in this class! Who cared if the maths was harder? Vanora settled into a seat in the far-left front corner. Once again her hair was wet and as she reached down to itch her ankle Rhiannon saw she wasn't wearing any socks with her lace up school shoes, which she would usually find gross but instead she found it... cool? Hot? What did she find it? Did she want to be friends with her or want to be her?

The maths teacher came in and immediately launched into logarithms and Rhiannon had to use all her brain power to keep up, to the point that by halfway through the lesson she had forgotten Vanora was even there, so didn't notice her as she walked out to use the bathroom (after asking first, of course). As she peed, she thought she could hear muffled sounds from the cubicle next to her, and as she washed her hands it was unmistakable. That was distinctly a sob.

'Hey, are you okay?' She stood in front of the final door. She didn't want to knock as well, in case it felt too invasive.

The sobbing got louder.

'Do you want to talk about it? Or do you want me to get you someone? I'm Rhiannon by the way. But you can call me Rhi.'

There was quiet. And then... the door slowly opened. Vanora sat on the lid of the toilet seat, eyes and lips swollen with tears, hair falling out of its bun. She looked at Rhiannon. 'Hey, I'm Vee. You don't have a cigarette by any chance, do you?'

'I don't, but I know where I can find one. Stay here.' She ran out of the bathroom and found Zoe's bag. As she rummaged for Zoe's tailors, she berated herself. '"Stay here" – where the hell was she gonna go? What a stupid thing to say.' She rushed back, half expecting the girl to be gone, but she was still there, though she had stopped crying.

Vee thanked Rhiannon as she took the cigarette from her, failed to light it with a shaking hand, then thanked her again as Rhiannon lit it for her. She took a long, deep drag, as though she were breathing in the sweet air of home after a long drive. Rhiannon noticed something strange about her; all of her fingers had little translucent webs of skin between them. Vee noticed her looking and said, 'They're webbed fingers. I was born with them.'

'Your toes too?' Rhiannon asked curiously.

In response Vee put the toe of her shoe down on the heel of the other and plied her foot out of her shoe. Her toes were pink and cute – and webbed. She lifted up her leg and wriggled them in Rhiannon's face, and Rhiannon could only wonder at becoming acquainted so quickly with so many parts of her. Parts that she now recognised she had thought about. Parts that she now recognised she was attracted to. She was attracted to Vanora. That was it.

She looked away, met Vee's eyes, looked away again. 'Sooo... what were you crying about? If you want to talk about it that is.'

'My period is late. And I'm worried I'm pregnant.'

'Oh. Fuck.'

'Yep,' she took another long draw.

'Have you had a pregnancy test?'

'No, I didn't have the money and I don't know who to ask. I don't want to ask my mum and I can't ask my dad...'

'Okay well that's easily sorted. My Centrelink came through on Friday so I can get it for you.'

'What – would you really do that?'

'Of course, don't even worry about it. I can get it in town before school tomorrow and I can give it to you on the bus. You catch my bus right?'

'Yeah, I do.'

So she had noticed her! Rhiannon felt a warm fuzz bloom inside her. She could feel her ears get hot and knew they were turning red under her hair. 'So that's all sorted then,' she said to cover her confusion.

'Unless I am...'

'Well, we'll cross that bridge if we come to it.'

Vee frowned for a second, and then beamed. She put out the cigarette on the top of the toilet paper dispenser, straightened her skirt with the other hand and then reached out to shake Rhiannon's hand with it.

'Thanks, Rhi.'

'You're welcome... Vee.'

After splashing water on her face in the sink, she turned to Rhiannon. 'How do I look?'

'Beautiful,' Rhiannon answered. And she meant it.

At recess she told the others that she had spoken to Vanora, though she didn't tell them the whole story. Zoe was in disbelief. 'I've been here for four years and never even got a hello from her.'

'She's probably so hot and cold that she'll blank you next time she sees you,' Cam said. Rhiannon was so high on the meeting that she hadn't even thought of this. For the rest of the day she was so anxious she could barely sit, waiting for the inevitable snub.

That afternoon, as she walked up the steps of the bus, she saw Vanora sitting near the front, in her usual spot. Rhiannon quickly looked away so she didn't have to make eye contact and face rejection. As she began to make her way down the aisle though, a tentative hand touched her shoulder. 'Rhi, do you want to sit with me?'

4

'Vee, Vee, Vee. It's all she ever talks about,' Ellie complained to her mum, as the latter readied herself for a Monday day shift.

'Don't be jealous, it's only going to push her away,' Sasha said as she rubbed sorbolene cream onto her whole body. Her skin was constantly dry, a side effect of her work and the endless showers it required.

'It's only natural for her to have a good friend at this new school. She needs to hang with someone. She still spends all her weekends with you.'

'Yeah, but I bet it would be with Vanora if she lived closer. All she can talk about is how *cool* and *amazing* she is.'

'She would think the same things about you.'

'Well, she doesn't *say* them does she?!'

'It sounds like she has a crush, and good for her.'

'A *crush*?'

'Has it never occurred to you that Rhi is gay?

'What – *gay*?!'

'Is it really that much of a shock to you?'

Simultaneously, Rhiannon was on the phone to Vee, asking her if she wanted to come and stay over on Friday night. Her mum was going to be gone for most of the evening at a book club, so they would have the place to themselves. She lowered her voice as she said this, knowing Angela would be listening. She wished more than ever that she could text Vee but her mobile got no reception at their house, and she never had credit anyway (and Vee, astoundingly, didn't have Myspace). Vee said yes without hesitation. Every day since her false pregnancy scare, they had sat together on the bus. They still didn't really hang out at school – they weren't in each other's classes besides maths and, Rhiannon soon discovered, Vee often skipped the class before lunch and caught a bus to the beach in the middle of the day, coming back only for the final period when attendance was marked – But oh, those forty minutes of bus ride each day! It was a hallowed time.

That week it rained and rained and rained. The Bellinger swelled and browned as it always did, and on Friday at midday the Bellingen bus was sent to pick up the kids early from school, before all the bridges went under. Vee left with Rhiannon, and the mood on the bus was one of elation. A year eleven boy hit on them both on the way home, came up to the front of the bus so he could lean over the back of their seat; 'come back to mine for a flood party,' he kept insisting.

'He just wants us to get flooded in at his house for a few days,' Rhiannon whispered.

'Hey, I heard that! What's so bad about being stuck at mine? It'll be sick. I'm on the side with no police and the bottle-o.'

'Dude, so am I. I'm out in Thora. It's also just so you have a chance to get with her.'

He opened his mouth to respond but no response came, and after a long minute he gave Rhiannon the finger, annoyed at her cock blocking, and skulked back to his seat alone. If Rhiannon felt any sense of rudeness that dissipated with the grateful and knowing grin that Vee turned on her.

They met up with Ellie in town, all of them grabbing a chai milkshake at the gelato bar together before catching the final bus home. Ellie watched the two of them flirt as she tactfully pretended to be interested in how big she could blow her bubbles. Now that she knew what it was she wasn't threatened – after all, *she* didn't want to get with Rhi! She was surprised by how much she liked Vanora, who was friendly and easygoing in spite of her mysterious reputation.

'Come stay at mine, it'll be so much fun. It looks like it's going to be a big one, we might even be stuck in till Monday.'

Rhiannon looked at Vee, fiddled with the straw in her mouth and considered. She knew she had a crush on her, she had accepted that. She knew she wanted nothing but to be alone with her. But she had no idea if Vee was interested. She slept with boys after all... and besides, her mum would be home now because the book club would most definitely be cancelled.

Ellie saw her hesitation and added generously, 'You guys can have the spare room.'

'Are you cool with us changing plans slightly, Vee? Ellie's mum is great. She's so chill, not like other parents.'

'Yeah, I'm down for whatever. I'm just excited to see my first flood up close.'

'Okay, done. Ellie, just make sure I remember to call my mum from yours.'

That afternoon the three of them put on gumboots and waded across the flooded paddock opposite Ellie's house. The cows had already been moved up the hill and the water swirled around their shins. As they drew closer to the Bellinger, they could see that all the castor oils and juvenile casuarinas along the riverbank were being pummelled by the flood waters, flexible trunks bent almost horizontal. Rhiannon thought of *Gone with the Wind*, and the bend of buckwheat, bowing to the inevitable. That's what all these plants knew to do, and humankind had learnt to mimic it, in the building of Lavenders Bridge with its collapsible railings. Ellie's horses stared and snorted at the rising river, not truly scared because they had seen it many times before, just having fun as the girls were, splashing each other in the shallows, out of reach of the mighty current.

'Let's go look at Summervilles Bridge too,' Ellie suggested and they set off gladly, though Rhiannon's ankles rubbed unpleasantly against the gumboots because her socks had been suctioned off her feet when water got in.

The Rosewood River was more exciting, because it was a smaller river with a shallower bottom, and that showed in the utter chaos of the waters. There was a huge wave where the bridge usually was, and big logs jammed in what they could only assume were the pylons.

'What's that crashing noise?' asked Vee.

'It's the boulders on the river bed crashing into each other. Each time it floods they get thrown around and the river takes a whole new shape. This is going to be such a big one, maybe even as big as that one two years ago that left all the flotsam in those casuarinas, see way up high there?' Ellie pointed at what looked like birds' nests of sticks half-way up the branches. 'That's how high it got.'

They pulled some loose, dead vines down from the nearby trees and threw them into the maelstrom to see how fast they would travel, or if they would be sucked underneath. 'I've never seen a river look so much like the ocean,' Vee said, and she was right in her comparison. Dark and turgid, the water was made of conflicting waves that crested and broke on top of each other, endlessly, little caps of white that frothed as if above shoals or beds of coral. It was violent like the sea could be, far more violent than the Bellinger, which moved as one huge force, and seemed somehow tamer even though you knew beneath the surface corpses of wallabies and trees were carried pitilessly.

'You've got something on your leg, Rhi,' Vee said, gesturing lazily, and Rhiannon looked down to see a tiny black thing crawling up her thigh, that stretched with its long body like a slinky, gripped her with its hungry toothless mouth.

'Goddamn leeches!' She flicked it off with her index finger and then twisted round looking for more. 'They're all over our boots, guys! Look!' Sure enough, there were multitudes climbing up their gum-boots, seeking out the warmth of a groin and the easy access to blood. There were even more on the wet rocks and branches around them, reaching high and sniffing blind, ready to begin their impressive worming feat. They unanimously decided it was time to go back to the house.

When they got back to Ellie's the frogs were so loud in the pipes, croaking and glorying in all the rain, telegraphing their hallelujahs and mating calls to their kind, that they moved upstairs to her room, even though Sasha was happy for them to take up the living room and watch a movie on the big screen.

'They're really going off tonight, hey,' Rhiannon said.

'Maybe they fancy your friend,' Ellie quipped, nodding at Vee who had plonked herself proprietorially across Ellie's bed.

'Huh?'

'She's talking about my fingers,' Vee laughed, unfazed, 'you might be right, though I tend to think I have more of an affinity for salt water, not fresh water animals.'

'Yeah, Rhi said you love to swim in the ocean hey.'

'I do. Every day.'

'Does your family also?'

'My dad surfs. My mum loves the ocean. But she doesn't swim much anymore.' Something in her tone changed and Ellie switched effortlessly to another topic. Rhiannon was disconcerted by how easily they got along, how Ellie had none of the uncertainty that she had with Vee, but simply ploughed onwards as if she were speaking to someone normal. Rhiannon knew she was hopeless by comparison, she almost felt like a 'tharn' rabbit in *Watership Down*, it was so much to take in that she was going to be alone with Vanora, not at school, and going to sleep beside her later that night.

'Do you have any pets, Vee?' Ellie stroked her cat, curled up on her bed, as she said this.

'No, I love them but my mum doesn't like kept animals. What's your cat's name?'

'Fanchette. Rhi suggested it. It's from some book she loves.'

'The Claudine novels, written by this French woman in the early 1900s. Her husband locked her up and forced her to write them and then published them under his own name. She was obsessed with cats.'

'Oh yeah, I know who she is, she was –' Vee started to say, but Rhiannon was on a roll, her tongue finally loosened.

'Amazing, right!'

'I was going to say bisexual,' Vee stated simply and silence settled on the room like a shroud, till even the cat stirred in its sleep, sensing the tension through the deep dreams of a feline.

Ellie got up to go downstairs, thinking it best to give the other two a moment alone. 'Do you guys want a drink before dinner? My mum won't mind as long as we only have one. I think I've still got that goon you left here, Rhi.'

They both nodded yes and as she left the room Rhiannon moved up on to the bed, so she could stroke Fanchette and be seemingly focused on her while she tried to work up the courage to say what she wanted to say. She started it again and again in her head, felt that her jaw was almost jarred with inertia, ran over the first words so many times that it became a refrain; so, so what, so what about, so what about you, so what about you are, so what about you are you –

'So what about you, are you bisexual?' She finally looked up, darted a quick glance at Vee.

'Yeah, I am. What about you?'

'Yeah, I am, I guess. I mean... I know I'm into girls.' ('I know I'm into you!' her mind cried.)

'Cool.'

'Guys, can you open the door for me? I don't have enough hands,' Ellie's voice, and then her body, came crashing in, as Vee calmly got up and opened the door. 'What does your mum do, Ellie?' she asked as she poured them all equal measures of goon. The smell of the cheap white wine turned Rhiannon's stomach. She remembered the last time they got wasted, and determinedly took a large gulp to quell the memory.

'She works as a receptionist at some office in Coffs. What about yours?'

'Mine doesn't work but my dad is a lawyer. What about your mum, Rhi?'

'She's a primary school teacher, but she only works part time at the moment. Oh fuck, that reminds me that I gotta call her from your home phone. BRB,' and Rhiannon raced out the door.

'She doesn't like talking about her mum much.' Ellie imparted this knowledge almost formally, as if handing over a grave circumstance to Vee that brought with it its own etiquette. 'She's a pretty intense woman.'

'That's all good, I get that, my dad is too. Well not a woman obviously, but intense,' and their eyes met in understanding as they smiled.

After dinner the three of them lay down on Ellie's bed to watch *V for Vendetta*. Rhiannon had, unsurprisingly, read the comic, having stolen it from the Bellingen Library the year before because she knew she wouldn't be able to bring herself to return it. She consoled herself with the fact that she had already read it more times than it had ever been loaned out. She sat between the two of them, self-conscious and as aware of the parameters of her body as your big toe is when you stub it – she *throbbed*. She felt every shuffle, every breath that Vee made. The other two chattered and crunched smarties over her head, bantered about the common nickname between the protagonist and Vee.

'V for Vixen.'

'V for... Ventriloquist.' Ellie looked smug with that one.

'V for Vagina!'

'Shhhh, guys. I wanna actually watch this,' Rhiannon put an end to their raucousness. Evie was reading the letter from Vivian, the height of the emotion in the film. 'God is in the rain,' Evie repeated with arms spread wide, and Rhiannon thought of the rain they had had the last few days, the way it healed the parched earth of Australia, the way the rising flood waters were a show of incomprehensible powers and a reminder of their own insignificance.

'Wait, I missed that, were they lezzies?' Ellie chimed in, desecrating the moment, and Rhiannon gritted her teeth angrily as Vee laughed, the irreverence!

Rhiannon's annoyance had dissipated by the time they all went to bed, Ellie alone in her room, and her and Vee slipping between the sheets of the spare bed in the guest room. She held herself like a board on her side of the bed, desperately wanting to be touched by Vee but not wanting to intrude unwanted. She felt stiff down to her very knuckles, though inside of her all of her blood pulsed as if it were alight and awake, nocturnal like the possums scurrying on the roof.

To Rhiannon, Vee appeared to have no such qualms, draping herself over her, chin resting against her shoulder and right arm across her chest. An arm that didn't stay still; as she spoke she fiddled with Rhiannon's hair, the collar of the t-shirt she had borrowed from Ellie, and eventually came to be tapping gently on her clavicle. Rhiannon answered every query with a 'Mmmm,' barely capable of saying more with her body so distracted. Her heart pounded in her ears and pussy as Vee's fingers fluttered down her breastbone, just inside the edge of her top, and stopped at the raised skin between her breasts.

'What's this?'

'It's a scar.'

'Can I see it?'

It was easier to do than talk. Rhiannon switched on the bedside lamp, softly dislodged Vee as she sat up and pulled off her shirt. A raised purple scar ran straight from her sternum to her navel. Vee reached out, traced her fingers down it, held them at the base momentarily. 'What's it from?'

'A star picket. Two years ago, after it flooded, Ellie and I were swimming in the river and were half swept over some debris. We didn't realise that some fence had been washed up there. It cut me open. I don't mind it that much. Ellie thinks it's hot.'

'It is.' Vee stepped her fingers up the scar one by one. She paused at Rhiannon's breast bone, pressed her hand flat against it, and then brushed her fingers slowly across Rhiannon's right nipple. Rhiannon's exhale filled the room.

'Wanna make out?' Vee met her eyes as she asked and smiled a wicked smile; Rhiannon could only breathe a 'yeah,' even quieter than her exhale had been.

5

Ten days later Rhiannon sat in the year ten area with Keira and Zoe, all three of them looking over their notes for the upcoming exams. The November sun was sweltering, Rhiannon could feel the steady trickle of sweat from her armpits, and her thighs stuck to the seat and each other in class. Sometimes she even came up with a damp patch on her skirt, which Vee would touch as she passed her by in the quad and jokingly say, 'You've been thinking of me.'

'I can't believe we actually have to do this, like it's such a fucking farce,' spat Zoe. The state government had recently announced that the School Certificate was going to be phased out in the next three years.

'Well at least we know it doesn't really matter then, it's just practice for the HSC,' Keira was pragmatic.

Rhiannon wasn't really listening, struggling to pay attention in the heat. She had rolled her shirt up and her skirt down so that her stomach was exposed to the sun, hoping a breeze would tickle it, though in reality she would probably just be left with an uneven tan. She left her sleeves down though, always conscious of the smattering of half healed cuts. She knew the others wouldn't mind – Zoe had noticed them in the first week when changing after PE, had said 'it happens to the best of us' and lifted her sport shorts to show the scars at the top of her thigh – but she had an intense fear of anyone seeing them, it was her private shame, kept as close as the fights with her mum.

Her mind wandered back to that weekend, flooded in at Ellie's with Vee. Ellie had been right, it was a big one and they ended up staying till late Sunday afternoon, when the rivers had fallen enough to allow Rhiannon to walk home, and for Sasha to drive Vee to Hungry Head. The aftermath of the flood was far less aesthetic, with layers of silt and water-logged branches crowding the bank, the casuarinas slowly pulling clear of the earth, like half-hearted flags weighed down with muck.

Rhiannon didn't mind though, she had eyes only for Vee. The square of her pale stomach beneath her tank top, the dimples of Venus above her Supré cut offs, the hair that she knew waited beneath them, as dark and twisted as her own adult fantasies. Used to the bare mounds of Tumblr porn, she found it the height of erotica; beautifully dirty and so, so personal; she wanted to tangle her fingers in the wiry hair and cup that epicentre of the other girl's being.

Vee was so fair that she had to sunscreen herself whenever she left the house, and Ellie had teased her ruthlessly.

'It's because my mum's Scottish.'

'Is she really?'

'Yeah, she's from the Orkney Islands. My dad met her there when he was doing a surfing trip around the UK and brought her back here.'

'Brought her back' was an odd use of words but neither of them commented on it, they were both intrigued by her having a mum from somewhere else with a different accent, and pushed Vee to do an imitation of some of Shrek's most iconic lines. She obliged and then deflected, asking Ellie where her dad was from.

'Oh Myanmar. But he and my mum were never together. I don't know him.'

'Was it a one-night stand?'

'Yeah, she only met him once. She was nineteen.'

Sasha had called them back up to the house then by tolling the rusted cowbell on the front porch. She was heading into Coffs for work and offered to drop Vee home on the way. Vee pulled Rhiannon around the side of the house while Sasha rolled a ciggie, and Ellie plucked cattails from their stems, the sudden give reminiscent of and as satisfying as pulling a hair from her brow, and left them to their privacy. It was the first time they had kissed in the full sunlight, and as their lips touched Rhiannon opened her eyes, to find that Vee's were open too and were the chocolate brown of a dog's, all liquid and docile. When Sasha called them to come to the car Rhiannon stepped back, touched her lips where she could feel the wet of the other girl's saliva, from where Vee's tongue had been just a moment before. Rhiannon then reached for Vee's hands to hold them between her palms, squeezed them to her and said, 'Your eyes are just like a seal pup's.'

Vee almost winced, gathered herself and then, reaching out to stroke Rhiannon's lips once more, murmured with a grin, 'I guess the flood method worked then,' mockingly referencing the failed advances of the year eleven boy before turning to go with Sasha.

Ellie leaped on Rhiannon with grasping fingers as soon as the car went down the drive; 'Rhiniiii what happened tell me everything!'

And Rhiannon had repeated it, both the nights, in a voice of excitement and disbelief, not with all the details though, not as she was remembering it now, all the cushy softness and tight ridges that closed around her hands, the way that Vee tasted like brine, had climbed up on her face so that she was left with the wet of her from cheekbones to chin, smeared across her skin so that she felt she smelled of the ocean afterwards. She didn't tell Ellie that Vee had ridden her mouth, tongue flat against her growing clit, with the same rhythm she had seen Ellie ride her mare at a canter, long smooth strokes as if she were polishing her past even the sliiide of the seat of a saddle. She didn't tell her that Vee had touched her so sweet that her voice had died in her throat, because everything was at that one spot inside her, and noises caught at her tonsils only to be tossed back down into the depths, till the only sound coming from her was from within, a squelching as Vee finger fucked her. She didn't tell her that she'd licked salt from Vee's underarms and thought it was delicious, that her tongue had traced her entire body so there was not a texture she didn't know. Those things she kept to herself, to take out and mull over when she was alone, admire the shine of them like Silas Marner when he counted his coins, treasuring with greedy hands that became greedy fingers inside of her, maybe she hoarded them under her floorboards too, because that's when she usually brought them out in the weeks afterwards, in bed at night when the moon glanced in her windows and the bats were amok.

'What are you thinking about?' Zoe asked, interrupting her recollections at school a few weeks later.

'She's thinking about Vanora again. You can tell by that look on her face.' They all knew about her and Vee now, that they were sleeping together or dating or whatever it was. Rhiannon sensed that maybe it wouldn't have had the same acceptance, completely without hesitation, if Vee didn't have such an aura of enigma and ease, that made people want to know her, in any way possible. Cam especially, both excited by an obvious gay couple and acutely aware that his new association with Vee raised his own social capital 'totally shipped it,' as he put it. Even with her relationship to Rhiannon, Vee was still largely elusive, preferring the company of the beach to the group, though she always joined them for recess now and sat with them in maths.

That lunch time she stayed with them, sitting in the shade cast by the demountables on the edge of the oval. Some boys in the year above kicked around a soccer ball on the field nearby, and one, a surfer boy from Hungry Head with a decided pout and a flop of sun-bleached bronze hair, waved at Keira.

'Is that Flynn waving at you?' Cam sounded almost incredulous.

'Yeah, we've been chatting on MySpace a bit,' answered Keira.

'A bit! They've been talking all the time and they're hanging this weekend,' Zoe said, accompanying it with an enthusiastic squeeze of Keira's thigh.

'Isn't he from out your way, Vee?' Rhiannon asked.

'Yeah.'

'Do you know him?'

'Na, not really.'

As she said that the ball was kicked in their direction and Flynn came jogging over to collect it. He gave a general hey, exchanged a few quick pleasantries with Keira and then, as he turned to go, acknowledged Vee with a jerk of his chin and a 'Hey, Vee', a use of her nickname that implied a greater intimacy than Rhiannon had expected, and one to which Vee didn't respond.

On the bus home that afternoon Rhiannon brought it up again; 'I thought you said you didn't really know him – it seemed like he knew you?'

'I guess he thinks he knows me; I don't presume to know him.' Unbeknownst to Rhiannon, Vee's mind swept back to an early morning at Hungry Head, sea slick and hungry. The tide was in and she had waded back through the lagoon. The water was stained dark brown by the tea trees, she had sat down in it and felt she bathed in warm iodine, did a few dolphin rolls and relished the warmth after the cold of the ocean, and when she rose from it he was there, watching her with his wetsuit rolled down around his waist and surf board in hand.

They often crossed paths at the beach, but that morning she looked at him and he looked at her, and she had felt her need drip down into the lining of her bikini, knew she hungered for more than food, her stomach not the only hollow crying to be filled, and so she beckoned to him and he waved uncertainly back and then she turned and splashed across the shallows, looked back to make sure he was following. In the damp sand beneath the tea trees she guided him into her from behind, standing on tiptoes to better take him, his chest pressed against her back. She twisted her neck to feel his mouth on hers, twisted her hand round too to take him out momentarily, feel his cock wet with her, and then let him plunge back in. As he got closer to coming he had knocked against her cervix, and she had wished it was a wall that could be broken down so she could take him into her lonely womb, use him as a furnace to heat her from within, fill the hollow need in her heart from the base up, have this feeling with her always so she never needed to seek it out.

Instead, he had come, and she had felt his sperm trickle out of her for hours afterwards, a pathetic ooze, and wondered if he had simply carved away more of her, so she was left even hungrier than before. Or wondered if all these flings, these beachside fucks, would eventually add up, the discarded carcasses of silly loves, and leather her whimsy, till she no longer chased person after person for a moment of solace. They didn't, but the resulting pregnancy scare had brought her to Rhiannon, and so maybe the coupling had set off something new in her life.

'Catch ya,' she'd shot over her shoulder as she left him trying to tug his wetsuit back on.

'Don't you ever get cold??' He'd asked, mesmerised by her swimming in a bikini in the dregs of winter, without the protective lard of a sea creature. 'Na, not really.'

When Rhiannon got home that evening Vee's reticence was pushed out of her mind immediately by the sound of the cows mooing, and as she switched into Crocs she swallowed her frustration at her mum, who said she had not been down to look at them even though she had been home all day; how she could ignore those plaintive sounds Rhiannon didn't understand. They had been mooing as she left to school in the morning too, but she hadn't had time to check on them before Angela dropped her at the bus, who told her they were sure to be fine when she mentioned her worry. They must have been really distressed to be still going ten hours later though, and so she set off to the paddock immediately, with Ajax following. The two Angus cows had both calved recently and had newborn black calves with doe eyes and swirls on their chests, cow licks that changed direction with their mothers' rubber-tongued care. When she arrived at the paddock, she could only see one calf though, and one mother stood at the fence line, rocking from hoof to hoof and lowing like a foghorn.

Rhiannon climbed over the barbed-wire strands at a fence post, where it was taut and could better support her weight, and began to walk the fence line. She could smell it before she saw it, and Ajax started to frantically run ahead, nose to the ground. There was the calf, flat on its side, small enough to be picked up in her arms. It was still alive, breathing faintly, eyes wide open and staring, froth at its mouth. It was too late though. It smelt like death. Its organs must have gone already. The poor thing was almost dead, dehydrated and starved, separated from its mother. It had been a hot day and it stood no chance at the age it was, must've curled itself up for a sleep close to the bottom wire of the fence, which was unbarbed, and stood up on the other side of it. It had probably walked the fence line through the night and morning, wearing itself out, not knowing how to cross back under – or over. She touched its little hoofs, perfectly formed and cloven, and its coat with the brown tint at the curls of the hair, the mark of the neighbour's Hereford bull who had sired it.

'Stuck on the wrong side of the fence,' she was terse with her mum.

'It's not my fault, I've been busy working on this stuff for school all day, have been chained to the computer, couldn't leave it, this new syllabus is too much and I need to pay for *your* school fees. Besides, grandma called, and you know how she is; it threw off my whole afternoon.'

'I wasn't saying it was your fault,' Rhiannon answered sadly. She was just as culpable, should've skipped school to check, was responsible for it in the way all humans who put up fences are for the animals within them. She knew couldn't trust her mother to watch out for them, her mother who had watched Ajax slaughter a chicken in a prolonged game in front of her, who had defended the dog by saying, 'he's just playing.' The poor hen, dead as a result of human negligence.

'It already smelt rotten,' she explained tearfully to Ellie on the home phone later, and she didn't have to explain anymore. Ellie, in the way of all country girls, had also seen animals pass before their time – red belly black snakes with spines severed by a slasher, a horse with a shattered shin groaning in a cattlegrid, a pademelon sickened with ticks dying slowly at the edge of the creek where it had gone for a final drink, a pup that couldn't suckle, that became stiff and silent.

Rhiannon slept and sweated with guilt, waking up from sleep paralysis to find the heaviness holding her down was simply the weight of a suffocating doona. The cow mooed ceaselessly and mournfully through the night.

6

'Why's your mum got a hotel room here?' Vee asked as she, Ellie and Rhiannon sat in the unnaturally warm resort pool in December, fake palm fronds dangling over their shoulders and bubbles shooting between their legs. They were at Aanuka, a resort on Digger's Beach, one of the more touristy beaches in Coffs Harbour, and Sasha had given them her spare key so they could get around. Having finished their year ten exams, term four had finished early for them, and the almost two months of summer holidays ahead felt infinite.

'Her boss got it as a perk from frequent flyer points so he let her have it for the day. She's got a bunch of work to do so she's just using the hotel room and making the most of the space away from me, as she says.'

'Should we see if Cam and Zoe and Keira wanna join?' Rhiannon asked. 'Careful. Three teenagers in the pool without parental supervision is already stretching it, we'll draw attention with six of us, don't want to get Ellie's mum in trouble.'

'Oh, it's fine.' Ellie dismissed Vee's cautiousness with a wave of her hand. 'How often do we get to do this anyway? Let's make the most of it. I don't have any credit. Who can call them?'

Rhiannon called and both Cam and Zoe said they'd come. Keira demurred, having plans with Flynn already – 'but I'll see all of youse tomorrow night at the doof right?'

Cam's older sister dropped him off, giving Zoe a lift on the way, and Ellie let them in through one of the gates and brought them along the winding garden path. Cam and Zoe were bursting with a story they could scarcely contain as they shed their clothes and slid into the pool. Their loud voices caught the ears of the relaxing adults stretched out on reclining chairs poolside, but the teens didn't notice the eyes on them, as they were half hidden behind dark sunglasses and lazily twitching palm fans. 'You'll never guess what we just saw when we picked up Zoe.'

The others scarcely had time to respond before he kept going. 'There was a fire at 190! And so all the prozzies had to run out and some were even in towels and there was even a chubby man who came out in a towel too. They all just stood around the car park at the entrance while the fire brigade came. Turns out it was a false alarm but it was so funny.'

'I don't get how that's particularly funny,' Vee said.

'Um, because it was a bunch of hookers around a parking lot with their tits falling out of their push-up bras and their toe nail polish chipped?'

'Come on Cam, we weren't actually close enough to see their toe nails,' Zoe corrected.

'I just don't see how laughing at women who maybe have no other option is funny,' Vee said.

'Oh, chill out! Prostitution is about the only job that's lower on the social scale than Maccas, which, can I remind you, I now work at two days a week, so if I want to make fun of them I can.' But he was put out, the humour sapped from the situation.

'You know what E B White said?' Rhiannon jumped in. '"Explaining a joke is like dissecting a frog – you understand it better but the frog dies in the process."' Rhiannon's peacekeeping tactic worked. They all laughed and teased her about her nerdiness and the harmony returned. They began to frolic about in the pool, doing handstands and duck dives and splashing and squirting water at each other with no concern for either the paying guests or the bacteria present. As Ellie came up from a tumble turn with water running out of her nose she saw a security guard headed their way.

'Shit! Someone must've complained about us. I don't want to get Sasha in trouble. Let's bail.'

They all scrambled out, grazing their shins against the side of the pool in their rush, grabbed their clothes and began to power walk along the edge of the pool at a pace that would have made Kel Knight proud. Hopefully the security guard would drop off and they could circle back. He seemed intent on following them, though, and as they got to one of the gravel tracks that wound its way through the resort he hopped on to a waiting buggy and began pursuing them.

'Are we like seriously being chased in a golf buggy?' Zoe gasped through laughter as they broke into a run.

He soon had them cornered at a double-barred gate, and with no other option in sight they began to climb over it. They had all clambered over to the street side by the time he pulled up, except for Ellie, who was perched on top of the gate, and he calmly walked over to the gate and pressed a button that began to open it electronically as she remained straddling it as it swung open, humiliated as her climb was unnecessary and too scared to jump down till it came to a stop. The guard just shook his head at their antics and said 'don't try coming back again today' as Ellie leaped down.

'As if we'd want to!' Cam said, loudly enough for the security guard to hear. 'Let's just go hang at the mall. That place was boring anyway.'

The next night Keira, Ellie and Rhiannon were in Ellie's room, getting ready for a doof near Ebor. They'd bought raspberry Absolut Vodka and caps in preparation, and organised a lift up with Flynn. Vee had decided not to come at the last minute, and both Cam and Zoe declined to spend their weekend in a mud pit with hippies with 'stomp sticks and rave shaves.' Sasha had offered to pick up Ellie and Rhiannon the next day, as Keira and Flynn were staying on two nights, sleeping on a mattress in his car, a mattress that Ellie and Rhiannon sat uncomfortably on top of on the long drive up the mountain.

'You don't mind your mum picking you up when you're legless?' Flynn was nonplussed.

'Na, she's the best. She even picked us up once at 2am when I was having a bad trip out the back of Kyogle, and that's a five-hour round trip.'

They had got the directions to the doof from a text message and so knew they had to drive about an hour out of Dorrigo into the bush, and as they tried to interpret the difference between a veer left and a turn left they wound down their windows and relied on their hearing to lead them to the property through the darkness. They could glimpse the headlights of other cars ahead on the usually empty country road which suggested they were going the right way and eventually they found a gate hanging off its hinges with a boy atop the post signalling to them; they each paid him their $40 entry and followed the muddy track down the hill that he directed them to. The girls were screaming with excitement by this point, the music getting louder with every metre. Flynn parked near a group of other cars and they began to slither and giggle down the two kilometres of slope, boggy from fifty or so cars that had passed down it earlier that day. It was pitch black, and they had only one phone between them to light up the worst of the holes, clutching their Norco milk bottles refilled with alcohol – there was a ban on glass – tight to them while shadowy figures leaned against cars alongside the bush track. Rhiannon and Ellie called greetings to people inside tents as they passed by, people prepared for the two-day haul with campfires and sitting areas covered with a tarpaulin. This was more their territory than Flynn or Keira's. Bello girls were raised on doofs.

'Oh my god I am so excited,' Rhiannon squealed as the dancefloor became visible, and the adrenaline began coursing through her. Two big screens were suspended either side of the stage playing a clip from *Fern Gully* and the eucalyptus surrounding the clearing were lit up with psychedelic colours – slashes of purple, orange, red and blue on their ghostly trunks.

'There's so many people,' she said, voicing all of their disbelief – how a deserted corner of a country property, fifty kilometres away from any town, could be transformed into a tribute to modern music while still somehow retaining its naturalness was beyond her. Here she was, stomping to prog, with bracken crunching beneath her feet, wait-a-whiles clutching at the hem of her dress and the crisp air of the Northern Tablelands, where it snowed in winter, filling her lungs.

The three of them sat down on a fallen log to drink some more before they went and danced, and revelled in the sights. There was so much happening – a girl came careening out of a lantana bush, lifting her shirt to show them the scratches she'd sustained on her back from fucking in it, a guy tried to sell them colloidal silver 'charged by the moonlight' from his boot, and in the car right next to them three people passed a bong round.

The door abruptly opened in their faces and Nat, a girl with a front fringe from Bellingen High, peered down at them. 'Want one, Rhi?' Rhiannon screamed in delight and flung herself across the log, flattening Keira and Ellie, to throw herself into Nat's arms.

'It's not that good an offer, it's just a baccy bong.'

'I just haven't seen you in so long!'

The two drunkenly cuddled for a bit and then Nat farewelled her friends in the car and pulled the others along to the dancefloor, by hand in a chain so they didn't lose anyone in the darkness (Flynn had been lost long before.) Ellie yelled something in Rhiannon's ear that she couldn't quite catch, and then stuck her tongue out at her. There was a cap sitting on it, and Rhiannon leaned in for the kiss, taking it into her own mouth as she did so. From that point onwards the night passed in a haze of dancing on speakers, stumbling into barbed-wire fences while trying to pee and skipping through the darkness, the amount of MDMA she consumed making her too ecstatic to walk.

When the sun began to rise people came pouring back onto the floor, and Nat ran out to them from the first aid tent. 'I passed out in there last night and I woke up cuddling this guy who had no teeth!' They laughed and dragged her down to the nearby creek. The water was icy cold but they all stripped off and waded in while psytrance played, and then shared cigarettes perched precariously on a rock. A boy was passed out a few metres away from them, and Rhiannon laughingly recalled that he had been there all night as she had vomited next to him at some point.

'We literally just danced nine hours straight,' Ellie said, with a satisfied sigh.

'Such a good night,' Rhiannon agreed.

'And we're going to do another nine hours straight. You guys want to get on board?' asked Nat.

'On board?' Keira asked.

'She means acid.'

'Fuck yeah, why not.'

Back on the dancefloor, Ellie's feet squelched in her Vans, which she had regrettably not removed when they had their morning dip. They went up to a white guy with dreads who, after being told what they wanted, said, 'ten dollars a drop.' He pulled out a bottle with an eyedropper and obligingly placed a drop squarely on each of their tongues – though Nat insisted on having hers on the back of her hand so she could ensure it was a decent-sized drop. They then wandered off to dance while they waited for it to kick in.

Some forty minutes later Rhiannon started to notice the hills were now moving separately like the cardboard cut-outs used in Balinese storytelling. Each time she turned towards the dancefloor there were myriad paths leading away from it that she had never seen before, but then she would see familiar faces stumbling along one and realise hey, she had been down there before, that led to the car! Squatting in the waist high grass with Ellie trying to pee, she could hear the urine rushing out and feel it down her legs but when she looked there was nothing there – this happened again and again till she finally asked Ellie to watch and tell her if she was actually peeing or not. Keira's calf muscle kept shortening and fattening till it was the exact proportion of a chicken drumstick and Rhiannon was practically salivating over it as they sat together at the edge of the dancefloor.

At one point they wandered back to Nat's tent and ate some pasta together – Nat enjoyed it so much she put her face flat into the container and the others grabbed pieces from all around her head. Rhiannon was unable to talk without speaking in the rhythm of the music.

'Does anyone want to go t-t-t-t-t-t-t-o the toilet?' she said, while everyone choked with laughter around her, Nat grabbing at her face with her hands trying to stop it from falling apart from laughing so hard, smearing the pasta sauce further down her neck.

The shadows from the branches of the trees made unending patterns of beautiful women dancing on the ground that Rhiannon could have happily watched forever. In one venture from the campsite to the dancefloor Rhiannon crossed Australia in four steps – she was weary, exhausted from her years of travelling and she paused for breath, struggling to lift her leg for the final step, overwhelmed by all those months of work and toil. 'I just crossed Australia. Wow.' But then she was back in northern New South Wales, not in Perth where she had crossed to, looking down at her bare feet which were far too hobbit-like, covered in mud from tramping in wet patches of ground.

At midday Ellie and Rhiannon began to climb the hill to the top car area to meet Sasha, who was bemused by their state. Ellie suggested a spontaneous road trip 'to anywhere right now! Because now is the time and I am so excited yes, so excited, this is going to be amazing! Let's stay out for days! Weeks! This will be great!'

'You've cooked it,' Rhiannon cackled.

They stopped at a petrol station on the way home for Ellie to pee, but she found the cubicle too terrifying – the toilet went down forever, straight down to the centre of the earth, she couldn't risk falling in, and so she climbed into the paddock next door instead and cried when the flock of sheep ran away from her, till Rhiannon cried with laughter at her crying.

'You two are a mess,' Sasha said as she rounded them up.

When they got home she made them cheese and avocado toasties and then sent them off to shower. While Ellie was in the bathroom Rhiannon looked for something familiar to comfort her; she picked up a book sitting on a shelf nearby, *The Wonderful Wizard of Oz*, and opened it to a random page.

'The four travellers walked up to the great gate of the Emerald City and rang the bell,' she read aloud – what?

'The four travellers walked up to the great gate of the Emerald City and rang the bell,' she tried again. 'The four travellers walked up to the great gate of the Emerald City and rang the bell.' Wow, that meant nothing to her. There were far too many subjects in that sentence – how could she hold them all in her head at once? 'The four travellers...' (she pictured the four travellers) '... walked up to the great gate...' (that one was hard, quite a few words in it, but eventually she grasped it after a few repetitions) '... of the Emerald City...' (she pictured the Emerald City) '... and rang the bell...' (she pictured the bell). Ahh, she'd got it! Well, that was exhausting. Quite enough reading for one day.

Ellie finally got out of the shower and Rhiannon went in. Her naked self in the full-length mirror was amazing. She twisted her hips on the pole of her centre and marvelled at how aerodynamic she was. But soon her nipples began to blur and become misshapen. Believing that this boded a sickness within, that warped nipples meant warped cells and therefore cancer, she felt a sudden fear and turned away from her reflection, not wanting to contemplate that possibility.

By two in the afternoon the girls' hallucinations had decreased in strength, and they lay side by side in Ellie's bed, going over all the events of the day and the night before. Rhiannon was absolutely exhausted and only wanted to sleep, but her mind would not allow her to rest yet – it still churned the sunlight into geometric women on the wall, that gyrated and swirled into still more columns of women, and the screaming of the cicadas transformed into psytrance with a drop and a rise and a drop and a rise and why wouldn't it stop!

As night fell and she closed her eyes, her mind filled to the brim with saturated colours and images of animals that folded into each other, a personal *Fantasia*. Vee appeared to her too, in a perpetual state of sixty-nine with herself, indistinguishable from each other as they were and incapable of being seen as the sole giver or receiver in her mind, they merged into a passive action similar to a tantric Buddhist wheel, unendingly circling. Then they became two leeches, twining around each other. Then Vee thickened, grew flippers where her webbed fingers usually were, Rhiannon shifted back to her human form and scissored her girlfriend's seal shape, Vee rubbing on her as if she were a giant clit with whiskers, tribbing away. Then she vanished, and in her stead there appeared a school of seals in Rhiannon's mind, rows and rows of them all bouncing balls upon their noses. Then, looking closer, she realised the balls were not in fact balls but versions of herself rolled up nude, rounded and grasping her knees, and each time she bounced downwards the seal's nose went up her cunt, which was wet and ready, tickled by the whiskers, the pyramid snout wedging further up inside her, so close now to making her orgasm, to making all of the hers finish. Should she touch herself while Ellie slept, was Ellie asleep, was she asleep, was this a dreamgasm she was having now, thighs tightening around her hand or a seal's eager nose?

7

Vee had got her red P's the second week of December, and it eased not only their relationship but Rhiannon's with Angela. Now she didn't have to beg or barter with her mum for lifts to places. Now Vee could come visit her and not be reliant on a school bus timetable. Angela had her book club on Fridays once a month and was always gone late, and they relished that time alone, their only intrusion being Ajax, who was intensely infatuated with Vee, always winding his lissom body round her legs in fascination, rolling and whimpering at her feet, offering his tummy up for her in subjugation, wanting to cling to her in the same way that delicious smell clung to her. They had to tie him to his rusted chain beneath the verandah or else he whined while they fucked and tried to wriggle his way between them. 'I've never seen him so excited; dogs must really love you,' Rhiannon had commented the first time, and Vee had said nothing back.

Vee drove round that balmy December evening and they smoked a joint on the verandah as the sun left the sky, illuminating the tip of McGrath's Hump before disappearing completely. It began to rain lightly, and they watched it shining in the darkness as they looked out across the empty paddocks. The silences lengthened, the shadows deepened and every touch was sensual. Rhiannon lay Vee back, nude on the trampoline, wet with dew, and ate her out with three fingers inside her. The scent of the jasmine was almost stronger than the scent of her cunt, that and the passionfruit flowers wilting white on the hedge beside them, which cordoned off the septic tank from sight and smell. She took forever to come, or not long at all, who could tell, Vee's sighs of pleasure going on into infinity, swallowed by the night around them.

Afterwards they shared another joint, and then the home phone rang. It was Ellie, asking if they wanted to go skinny dipping at Summervilles Bridge now that the clouds had cleared and the moon was out. They dressed themselves slowly in the half light cast by the lamp from the living room that glanced into Rhiannon's bedroom. Then Vee drove them to pick up Ellie and take them all back to the bridge, with her right hand on the wheel and her left stroking Rhiannon's clit all the while, so that Rhiannon kept giggling and answering 'nothing' when Ellie demanded to know what she was giggling about. As they stepped into the river all three of them grabbed at each other, losing their balance on the rocks and cackling.

'I'm too high for this,' Rhiannon said, but she meant too horny. She could hardly concentrate, and as she paddled under the bridge she could feel something stroking her legs, and she opened them wider thinking it was Vee.

'Something keeps touching me,' Ellie said.

'It's just the silkiness of the currents,' Vee reassured her, and it occurred to Rhiannon that perhaps she was initiating a threesome, touching Ellie just as she was touching her. That was an absurd thought though, and she threw it from her mind.

After some time they got out and stood, naked and dripping, on the bank. Vee turned on her headlights so they could roll another joint, and that's when they saw the river was swarming with eels, lithesome bodies oscillating till you couldn't tell where one ended or another began. They had been them rubbing against them, wrapping around their legs, brushing on their most private parts. Rhiannon and Ellie both squealed, but Vee shushed them with a 'they're harmless, they would've hurt us already if they weren't' and Rhiannon wondered if she'd known all along.

The next day they spent the day with Ellie and rode her horses bareback down to the creek near Rhiannon's. Ellie and Rhiannon double-dinked on Gemma, and Vee was put on the old bay quarter horse, Ludo. They trotted up the creek, the water was chest deep and splashed up on to them as the horses' hooves churned the pebbles and turned the clear creek brown. Then they let them graze in the long grass beside the bank, reins tied out of reach of their legs, as they pulled off their denim shorts to swim in their bikinis.

Vee had horse hair all up her inner thighs, looked like some sort of werewolf chick, a mythological hybrid stepped out of history, and Ellie apologised for the gelding, 'he's always moulting,' but Vee just wiped it off unbothered.

After swimming they sat in the shallows, watched tadpoles gather around their toes, nibbling at the skin on their feet, and yarned about river stories. Rhiannon told the tale of the time she got stung by a bullrout, those fish with venomous spines, and her hand swelled to three times its size, and she screamed the whole way to hospital and had her hand thrust into a bucket of boiling hot water by the nurses, because that was the only thing that could ease the excruciating pain.

A kingfisher watched them from a low hanging bough as Ellie plucked bullrushes, spliced them in the gap of her teeth, only to look up and realise the turquoise bird wasn't the only thing watching them.

'Rhi, that guy is there again.'

There he was, naked in a break in the trees, with a hard on, staring at them, completely composed and completely unashamed.

Rhiannon groaned. 'Let's go,' she said, and they mounted the horses and went back up the bitumen road, not even bothering to pull their shorts back on in their rush to leave, just holding them in their hands along with the reins. The clip-clop of the horses' hooves as they put space between themselves and him soothed them more than anything they could say to each other.

After dinner Vee drove her and Rhiannon to her place, along Short Cut Road, past the faded beach motels of Urunga with rabbits leisurely cropping the lawns, and left at the Hungry Head sign, which marked how many kilometres it was to the beach. 'Hungry 4 Head? That's so funny.'

'Yeah, it's an unfortunate placement, hey but I love it... this is the second time they've had to replace it; people keep nicking it.'

The country was more open than what Rhiannon was used to. Neat groves of planted trees and two dams lined the roadside at the lead up to Vee's driveway, and grey kangaroos gathered in the last rays of the sun, kangaroos that would be too large for the dense rainforest around Rhiannon's own home. Vee said the bird life was mainly pee wees, magpies and butcher birds; she liked to feed them from their porch. The neighbour's paddock had some nesting plovers that swooped you though, and of course 'there were all the coastal birds still.'

'Oh, and,' she added, seemingly as an afterthought, 'just so you know, my mum's always drunk.'

They pulled up to the house and Vee's dad, Paul, came out to meet them. He was friendly, welcoming Rhiannon with a hug. She wondered momentarily what her own life would be like with two parents at home, with one to cushion the conflict with the other, to maybe even be a punching bag for you, to divert some of the attention off of you. Like Angela, he didn't seem to notice anything different about her and Vee's friendship, didn't realise they were together. She supposed they were both obscured by and safe in their femininity.

'Your dad's so nice,' she said to Vee as they stepped inside.

'Sure, he seems that way,' Vee rolled her eyes and Rhiannon didn't question further, understanding immediately that there could be a discrepancy between what parents presented to guests and how they behaved behind closed doors.

'Vee, is that you?' A figure raised itself from the couch and as Rhiannon's eyes adjusted to the house after the outside glare, she saw a woman who once would've been beautiful, with the sharp cheekbones and dark features of Vee's but had skin desecrated by excessive alcohol consumption; deep lines, broken capillaries in her eyes and nose, water retention that thickened her jowl.

She rose to her feet and came to greet her daughter and the newcomer, and as she got closer, Rhiannon could smell the sour stench of whisky and see its effects in her sway.

'Rhi, this is my mum Isla; Isla, this is Rhi.'

'Short for Rhian would it be?' Her accent wasn't one Rhiannon had heard before, it had a Scandinavian lilt that she couldn't recognise, and she realised how ignorant it had been of her to ask Vee to do Shrek's accent.

'Rhiannon.'

'Ahh, a gorgeous name. Would you want a drink?'

'Nae, Mither, we don't want one. Beuy, lay back down you're knackered,' Vee helped her back down tenderly, and Rhiannon was surprised to hear what she could only assume was some kind of dialect.

They went to Vee's room, watched *Dangerous Liaisons* and were amazed by Uma Thurman's young breasts. Vee clamped Rhiannon's mouth shut with her hand as they quietly fucked so no sound gave them away, and they later emerged in pyjama shorts and t-shirts to brush their teeth before bed.

As they walked down the hallway, Rhiannon chattered away, feeling far more comfortable there than in her own home. 'Now that you have your licence we should go away together for a few days. How about down to Seal Rocks? Ellie says it's so nice.'

There was a kerfuffle from the couch, what sounded like a glass being knocked over, and Isla leaped up unsteadily, blankets slipping from her shoulders. 'Seal Rocks?' She exclaimed. 'Nae, dinnae go there. The poor selkies,' and she began to cry, fat tears visible on her cheeks in the gloom.

Rhiannon was speechless, mortified that she had somehow caused such a response, but Vee stepped towards Isla resolutely and put her arms around her to comfort her.

'It's Pet Porpoise Pool you're thinking of, Mither. We're not wanting to go there.' She turned to Rhiannon. 'We went to Pet Porpoise Pool once,' she explained, 'and it really distressed her. All those sea animals locked up in those tiny pools, forced to perform.'

'Ahh yeah, it's awful,' Rhiannon agreed, wishing she had more to say, some consolation to offer.

'She's talking about the beach down south that we went to Mither, the one that had no seals, remember, just the name,' and she eased her back down again, as Isla's sobs began to lessen. 'We were very disappointed that there were no seals, weren't we Mither?'

'I miss the selkies,' she crooned.

'That's the Orkney word for the seals,' Vee clarified to Rhiannon.

'I miss us lyin' on the rocks of Birsay, warmin' wursels in the sun. I wish I had never gone to the bay that day and met your fither.'

'Hush Mither, it's been done,' Vee pulled the blanket up around her and then beckoned to Rhiannon to follow her back to her room.

'She's homesick. So sick for it she gets upset and confused easily,' she apologised to Rhiannon.

'No that's okay, I totally understand. Why doesn't she go home for a visit?'

'She can't. Let's go to sleep,' Vee hopped into bed and made space for Rhiannon beside her, pulled her against her under the covers. Just when Rhiannon thought she had fallen asleep she muttered, rancour evident even in that lowered tone, 'My father won't let her.'

As Rhiannon's mind drifted off into dreamland, with her girlfriend's arms comfortingly tight against her chest as they spooned, Vee's grew sharper with indignation, till she worried her angrily beating heart would wake the girl next to her. She felt as if the whole house could hear it shouting in the dark, the night around them was so quiet. She played a recent confrontation with her dad over and over again, from both her own point of view and her mother's – who she knew had watched from inside the house, concerned eyes peering out from the familiar shade into the glare of the backyard, seeing them exposed, by both words and sun.

'Why can't you just let her go!' Vee had screamed at her father.

'She might die!'

'She's dying already –'

'That's not certain. Letting her go is... besides, she's still my wife, and I love her. You can't understand that. But I love her for what *was*, what we *had*.'

'You can't keep her just as a way of holding on to that memory when it's at her expense, it's cruel. It's *possessing* her.'

'I'm *protecting* her from herself.'

'That's just patriarchal.'

'Don't cite terms at me you don't understand, Vanora. This is all beyond you. She's all that's left of what we had.'

'You're keeping her as a relict.'

Her breathing was heavy as she reached the crescendo and beside her Rhiannon twitched in her sleep, sensitive to the mood around her, permeating through her unconscious mind. Vee released her and rolled away from her carefully, and brooded on memories like a toad on a hen's egg, welcoming the dank of a basilisk or vengeance coming forth, anything to alter the state of the now.

The next evening Rhiannon found herself back out in Bellingen with Nat and Ellie. It was a Sunday night, but a Sunday night in high summer with schools out and the date pushing up against New Year's Eve, and so the town was busy. They sneaked into the local tavern by the back door, a friend in year twelve opening it for them, and danced among all the drunk oldies. They watched amused as a man got kicked out for pulling a snake out of his shirt ('how many times have I told you not to bring her to the bar, Dave!' the bartender yelled). At midnight, when the tavern closed, they wandered down to the goon shack alongside the river and Nat took out a small plastic Ziploc bag full of MDMA crystals. Her older brother was a dealer so she was always set up. 'Youse wanna? It's $20 for a point.'

Why not? The night was young and there was nothing else to do. They ate the MDMA and then crossed Lavenders Bridge back to the skate park, lay back in the bowl on their backs, listened to the flow of the Bellinger as they came up, talking excitedly and bursting into fits of hugging.

'I'm *so* glad we're friends,' Ellie said over and over again as Rhiannon slid down a skate ramp on her belly.

'Hey, you guys have to feel this, it feels incredible,' Nat called them back to the bowl where she ran her hand up and down the side, the concrete pristine and soft between swathes of faded graffiti, commemorating skaters and locals of the past. 'Your skin feels amazing too,' Rhiannon said and soon they were all caressing each other's arms, the skin of their stomachs, the raised scar that ran down her torso, glorying in all that body and all those nerves. Nat took off her top to be able to rub her breasts against the wall of the bowl, and then they were both kissing her breasts, and taking turns to kiss each other.

'This feels *amazing*,' they repeated like a mantra. It felt completely non-sexual, just delighting in the wealth of senses available to them, and in her euphoric state of mind Rhiannon didn't care what Vee or anyone else would think. Like Felix Felicis, MDMA tells you that it is the right thing to do at the right time.

When they felt glutted on their orgy of feeling, Nat pulled her top back on and they began to walk up the incline to the main street. They stopped at every lamp post to marvel at the clouds of Christmas beetles, a miasma around each light. When they reached Church Street they found a bunch of drunk 'deros' in hoodies lighting up the community noticeboards. The papers and cork flamed satisfyingly, but faltered at the brick surrounds.

'Oi, Nat,' a boy yelled, from the branch of a camphor laurel where he sat overlooking the night time activities.

'Heyyy, Jason!'

'Can you tell me if the Swiss Patiss is open yet?'

'Sure.' Nat walked towards the bakery. It was 3am, but the baker started early, to be open by 6am, and sometimes he would open his doors for the drunk teenagers to purchase things in the wee hours.

When he learned it was open Jason clambered down the trunk, went into the Swiss and came out with two pesto snails.

Nat looked at them hungrily. 'Jason, give me a bite.'

'Naaaa.' He looked her up and down, then reconsidered. 'All right then, maybe, if you give us a pash, I'll give you a whole one.'

She looked at Rhiannon and Ellie, and they both shrugged unconcerned, they wouldn't judge her. What was one pash anyway? They were all just making out with each other.

She stepped towards him. 'Deal.'

After they pashed the three of them meandered back to the north side, leaving Jason behind as Nat tore up the snail with her hands rather than her teeth as they walked. Nat's house was near the showground, and Ellie insisted on a detour to look at the horses agisted there, though Rhiannon moaned that they could hardly even see them in the dark so what was the point? They could hear their quiet snuffles and teeth tearing the clover though, and that was enough for Ellie. She was one of those horse girls that dreamed of supple leathers and sparkling bits hanging up on a wall as if it were jewellery, as Velvet Brown did before her Grand National win.

Back at Nat's they cuddled in her bed, shut down her suggestion to smoke some salvia from her back garden – Nat was always keen to push every experience to the limits – punched some cones instead to take the edge off their comedown, and struggled to sleep before sunrise. They would feel awful tomorrow but who cared, they had nothing to do; could simply roll from bed into the river, float in the inflatable inside of a tyre, feel the peace of limbo with their School Certificate done and year eleven to come, on the brink of adulthood but not yet fretting at the future, it was a way off still, as unreachable as the Great Dividing Range on a 40-degree day, heat mirage blurring its features till it could be the smudge of an oil painting. There was all the time in the world.

8

'What about this dress? It's only $20,' Ellie smoothed the sun bleached 1950s cotton over her hips as she stepped out from the op shop change room.

'Well, that's a nice frock!' Cam was encouraging.

'Frock, who says frock?! LMAO,' said Zoe.

'Um, it's obviously vintage so that word's appropriate. Besides, who says LMAO anymore, Zoe, that's so 2007.'

'It looks good,' Rhiannon said. She moved between them, adding, 'But would you ever wear it?'

'Na, I guess not. But I just want to go home with something new!'

'Wow, that flood money is really burning a hole in you guys' pockets, hey.' Vee surveyed them languidly from a tattered couch, conveniently placed in front of the change rooms presumedly to facilitate the tired husbands and children who were dragged along and consulted on purchases, having resisted Rhiannon's attempts to pull her into the change room of Vinnies for a make out sesh.

'Flood money?' Cam asked.

'Me and Rhi both got a $1000 disaster relief payment from Centrelink coz of the last flood,' Ellie explained.

'Wait, what – were you even hurt?'

'Well no, but like fences were damaged and we missed school and stuff and I guess we got it coz of where we live.'

'Don't you worry, I've got another like five op shops to take you to yet, so you'll defs find something to spend it on. And if not, you could always lighten your load by chucking some my way...' Zoe joked as she walked away from them up the aisle, flicking through the racks as she did so.

She had offered to take Ellie and Rhiannon on their first exploration of the Coffs Harbour op shops in the first week of January. Being a low socio-economic area with a bit of a religious presence, there were a bunch in the central block of town, all 'chock full and cheap as,' as Zoe said. Vee, who despised shopping, had been roped into driving them there.

It was a hot day and as they squeezed their sweaty feet into second-hand shoes and filled plastic carry bags with clothing that left marks on their tired arms, their pace slowed, till at the fourth store, when Rhiannon broke out into an allergic rash from a questionable flounced item that no one could recognise what part of the body it was meant for, they all called it quits.

'Fucking dust mites,' she said, looking down at the red dots on her calves. 'You still look good to me, baby,' Vee said and, in a rare moment of public affection, kissed her on the cheek. Rhiannon looked up at her in surprise. 'Let's go. I'm sick of Coffs.'

Swinging her car keys, Vee led Ellie and Rhiannon back to the car park. She had a Commodore, which her dad had given her as a combined birthday/Christmas present, which Rhiannon referred to as her 'getaway car' in reference to *Two Hands*, the iconic Heath Ledger film that Rhiannon and Ellie both loved. Heath Ledger, the only celebrity death that had shook either of them, had left Rhiannon crying when it came up on the Ninemsn homepage, unsettling her on an intended foray on to the *PostSecret* forum.

As they hit the Pacific Highway, Vee speeding a calculated 6km/hr over the limit allowed by her plates, Rhiannon wound down her window, let the wind whip round her hair, gazed up at the cloudless blue and had a shock of euphoria. Here she was, with her best friend and the girl she loved, on a perfect summer day. She began to sing to herself, nonsense notes that were whisked out the window, unheard by the others. She wanted to dance, to scream, to get fucked up, all from sheer joy, couldn't contain it, and so held her hand out the window and began to wave it up and down as if it were riding the currents, wished she could surf them too, wanted to be hurtling hard and fast and maybe even blindly who knows where just somewhere, wanted to be like that guy in *Into the Wild*, just chasing adventure, wanted to be...

'Stop doing that hand thing. It's so fucking lame,' Ellie suddenly said, interrupting her reverie, before asking Vee, 'What's the plan? Are you just dropping us in Thora or are you gonna hang?'

'I'm just gonna drop you.'

'Wait, what? I thought you were gonna stay over!' Rhiannon couldn't disguise the disappointment in her voice.

'Na I've gotta spend some time with my mum. I haven't seen her much lately and I usually spend most of my school holidays with her.'

Rhiannon didn't argue, knowing Vee's reason was only considerate, but she felt sick at the thought of being alone with her own mum. She loved her home but her life there was one of avoidance. Sitting in the cow paddock at night to escape the trap of the house. Getting to the kitchen by walking out the back door and around the backyard, so as not to pass through the lounge room that was her mother's lair. Keeping her eyes down and her sleeves pulled low whenever she had to shuffle through, trying not to give her any entry into a conversation.

Ellie, sensing this, offered, 'You can stay at mine.'

'Yeah maybe I will. My mum wants me to be home for dinner, but I'll ask if I can come over after that.'

When she got home, Angela was on the phone to her mum, and she could hear her exasperated replies. Rhiannon knew she would have no chance getting an amicable answer to anything after that. She tried to keep things calm through dinner by tactically offering up town gossip, so her mum would sink her teeth into that rather than her daughter. Afterwards she shut herself in her room and binge watched *The L Word* that she was renting one disc at a time from the video store, on her laptop. She was excited by her newfound gayness, wanted to absorb absolutely everything she could of lesbian culture, had splurged on obscure Yuri manga, frequently checking the rusted metal dairy bottle letterbox for its delivery. She had tried porn but it didn't do much for her; she preferred the more fantastical world of Harry Potter fanfic, or the perfection of anthro art. She snuck her hand into her undies as *The L Word* ended and fished up some examples she'd saved from DeviantArt, lionesses with rippled abs and heavy breasts, either standing upright with legs twisted around a stripper pole or standing spread over a svelte zebra, which was bent on hocks and hooves, fawning at her paws.

    She worked away at herself, wiping her hand on her headboard after, felt it was even luckier than her usual obsessive and ritualistic rapping on it before sleep. Surely 'touch wood' warded off even more when wet with cum? She couldn't get back that high of the drive home though, felt suffocated by the other presence in the house, wondered what it was about her or her mother that made the air of the space shiver. Did Angela carry some sort of chemical that reacted with her own? Even her breathing at night set her on edge, whereas when Sasha entered a room with Ellie and her the atmosphere remained unchanged. Ellie was as relaxed with her mum there as she was with just the two of them, and there was no chill or tension in the aftermath either. How was that possible? She complained to her mum of period cramps and was tended to with a hot water bottle, whereas Rhiannon hand washed her underwear in the laundry sink so Angela wouldn't even have insight into her cycle, knew that something about her womanhood menaced her mother. She couldn't understand their intimacy.

    One time, though, she got a taste of what it must be like. Ellie had fallen asleep during a movie and Sasha had called Rhiannon into her bedroom while she readied herself for a date, said 'come chat to me.' Rhiannon had sat on the edge of the bed as Sasha put on make-up in the mirror and brushed her hair, the strokes a soporific ASMR. She hadn't asked questions, just talked easily, as if Rhiannon were a contemporary, not an untrustworthy young girl that was hiding things from her and had to be found out. It was a simple and brief moment, lasting maybe twenty minutes, but she still played it in her mind two years later, intoxicated by it.

Two days later Rhiannon awoke to a red sky. Her mum had gone into Coffs for the day and so she was left alone to meander down the road, puzzled by the colour. It wasn't bushfires, didn't smell like smoke, didn't have any smell at all really. It veiled the familiar hump of the Great Dividing Range as if she were viewing it in sepia, and the morning dew on the spikes of the Bunya pines sparkled with an orange hue, the same hue as the hump of Tall's back as he grazed. She was so used to curious natural events, having seen the valley she lived in distorted by rain and fog and heat haze, knew the way the white cedars two-toned leaves flipped in a storm, reflecting the mood of the wind, knew the green tinge that boded hail, knew the way the sun set on a glum day, steel greys and melancholy blue, that this just seemed another of mother earth's fickle displays.

She played with Ajax in the pipes that passed under the road where it crossed over the creek, hid in the trickle till he found her, his triumphant bark echoing in the concrete. Pelted him with Lilli Pillis, fell into a patch of stinging nettles and swore profusely, disturbed a platypus by the secluded swimming hole, stared at the strange sky in silence and then heard, oh so faintly, the ring of the home phone.

'Come on Ajax, we can make it!' she yelled as she sprinted back to the house, trying to grasp his tail as he drew ahead of her, hoping he could miraculously pull her up the hill.

She got it mid-final ring, cradled it to her chest momentarily as she tried to get her panting under control, and then answered it with her phone voice.

'Rhini, it's me, how hectic is this dust?'

'Oh, is *that* what it is?' And other people were experiencing it, it wasn't just some magical private immersion, her valley was a part of a wider world.

'Yeah, it's a dust storm blown from out west, Sasha told me.'

'How does she know?'

'She googled it. It's all over like Sydney too, apparently.'

'Oh, right. That's crazy,' she said, having no real concept of Sydney and knowing Ellie didn't either.

'Wanna come over?'

'I don't know if I can be bothered to walk, let's just talk on the phone. One sec, let me just get comfy.' Rhiannon pulled off her dress as she said this and pulled the trampoline around so that she could lie on it and the phone cord would still reach, fully stretched out.

'Okay now I'm sunning myself.'

'Naked?'

'Of course. Do you reckon I can still get a tan in this?'

'I don't know, maybe you'll get a sprinkle of dust on you, like a true Australian lamington; dust from the droughts.'

'Like a true Australian treat you mean.'

'Totes. By the way, what's happening with Keira and Flynn? Are they like together?'

'Oh yeah for sure, it's been official for a while I think...' her thoughts drifted to Flynn's unexplained recognition of Vee, and her mysteriously guarded response. She didn't distrust Vee as such, but she had never told her who she thought she may have fallen pregnant to, said it didn't matter, that it was just a one-time thing.

'Rhi?'

'What, sorry, I was zoned out. The sun is making me sleepy.'

'I was just saying I'm actually so excited for us to all go to school together, and us to catch the same bus again.'

'Me too!' Rhiannon forced herself to concentrate on the present conversation. 'It's going to be annoying, though. We finish later and by the time we get back to Bello the last Thora bus has already left... like, our mums are gonna have to pick us up every day.'

'I would say we could just give you a lift but Sasha will probably take us home by north side so she can –'

'I know I know, it's all good.' Rhiannon cut her off, not wanting Ellie to know how ideal that would be, to not have to spend twenty minutes in the car with Angela. The car was the worst place of them all, because there was no way out while they shot along Waterfall Way, and it somehow always turned into a listing of her faults, her mother alternating between lachrymose and vitriolic. The quieter Rhiannon got the more frenzied her mother became, till Rhiannon sunk into a sideways slouch against the window, her eyes unfocused on the blur of green, her ears unable to staunch that torrent, felt it break against her shoulder and cascade into her soul, wished she were the huntsman hanging on for dear life on the outside of the window, battered by other forces just please not this one enough please stop speaking I'm not those things you think I am, she couldn't say that though, what if it escalated it, and so she leaned as far away as she could in that tight space, gripped the door handle ready to leap out as soon as they parked, pictured the razor in her mind, knew what solace awaited her in that jewellery box in her bedroom, what shimmered among the necklaces she never wore, knew that soon, in fifteen minutes, in ten minutes, in five minutes, she would be calm, as calm as she seemed now in her misleading stillness, where only the flickering of her pupils showed any sign of life, stiff as if she had somehow entered rigor mortis, a disassociation that brought her relief, just as the little death of an orgasm did.

Her mother had been more difficult lately. The school counsellors had told her that Rhiannon was cutting, even though she had asked them not to tell her. They had insisted, when in the final week of term she had shown up with an infected arm after Zoe had talked her into going, not knowing what to do about the crusty pus that stained the inside of her school shirts. Angela had got it into her head that her daughter was being sexually assaulted, as the counsellors suggested that was what self-harming was usually evidence of, damaged goods, and she could believe it herself, already suspicious of signs she interpreted as hypersexuality, and so she sprang the topic on Rhiannon at any moment, supposing she could surprise an answer out of her.

'I know you're being sexually assaulted. Who is it?' greeted her at any point of the day, but most often in the car, and so Rhiannon had stayed home for long stretches of the summer holidays, refusing lifts into town because she didn't want to be cornered again, only going where she could walk or when Vee could pick her up.

How could she say, to the person that scared her the most, made her feel more powerless than anyone, that it was her that she hid from? That it was the deep unhappiness of her home situation that led her to harm herself? That would only leave her more exposed. So she stayed silent.

9

'What do you think she's thinking about?' Ellie gestured at Fanchette who, front paws rolled beneath her, peered with a contemplative expression out the window across the horse paddock. Like all cats she kept her secrets close, tucked like the tail around her haunches.

'She's thinking about her third name,' Rhiannon answered automatically.

'What?'

'Come on darling, keep up, it's a TS Eliot reference,' Sasha chimed in from the kitchen. 'I read it to you so many times as a child – the naming of cats –'

'– is a difficult matter. Okay okay, I remember now. You know I was always more into the horse stuff. Speaking of, wanna come help me clean the tack, Rhi?'

'Ummmm, not particularly.'

'Come on, it's like therapeutic. The smell of the saddle soap is so good. Pleeeeease,' she begged, dragging at Rhiannon's hand till she succumbed and walked out the door with her.

They strolled down the slope, stopping to pick at the pink sour flowers scattered among the emerald kikuyu as they went. They competed to see who could handle eating the most in one go, squishing the stems between their teeth to release the sourness that was on par with a warhead – if you were willing to eat enough. They reached the weatherboard shed that served as both tack room and feed room and they both inhaled sharply as they stepped inside.

'God, it really does smell so good,' Rhiannon said, as she began to lift the huge wooden lids one by one, to plunge her hands into each delicious textured bin, which was lined with tin to stop mice gnawing their way in and raiding the horses' feed. 'What are they all again?'

'Lucerne chaff, oaten chaff, barley, and that's for the birds of course,' Ellie added as Rhiannon submerged her arms up to the pits in a barrel of seeds. Sasha had an aviary out the back of the house where she rescued discarded breeding birds from pet shops. Cockatiels and budgies and lovebirds that had spent their whole lives indoors in cages got to spend their final years in an outdoor aviary big enough to fly in. It was almost a religious moment when Sasha released them into there, 'enough to make you believe in God' as she said; the birds would hold on to the mesh and stare for hours, in awe of such a big world, so green, so full of things that perhaps they'd somehow felt existed somewhere, heard in the chirrups of other birds or seen in their collective subconscious.

'Can we have some of that sweet stuff again?'

'The molasses? Yeah sure, just use that glass on the shelf there.' Ellie turned on the tap so that the treacle languorously oozed out, permeating the entire room. Once Rhiannon had satisfied her sweet tooth, they began to carry the tack out into the sun so they could oil it in the open air. On her second load Rhiannon looked up at the awning and started. 'Ellie! There's a snake's tail coming out of the edge of the roof!'

'Oh yeah, that's the diamond python. He lives up there and gets all the rats and mice. Pretty easy life for him really.'

'I thought Fanchette caught them?' Rhiannon had seen their conical noses, a standing testament to the cat's prowess, left in the hallway outside Ellie's door as a gift. Sometimes even decapitated, strewn bodies if Fanchette had already eaten her fill.

'She catches the ones around the house, I think this is his territory.' They placed the saddles over the gate and began to rub the stirrup leathers with tea towels so stained with grease that you could never determine their original colour. Ellie was right that it was therapeutic. Rhiannon found herself getting into a rhythm, especially as she reached the bridle and ran her cloth down the reins, feeling the leather grow more supple in her hands.

'So, should we go to that party tomorrow night?' Ellie said, breaking their reverie.

'Yeah, for sure, I mean it's the last party of the holidays, we can't miss it.' Rhiannon had her hands under the tap, scratching the congealed grass off a bit. 'I gotta see my dad in the afternoon but after that let's do pres.'

'Oh I forgot you were seeing your dad! What's he doing here again?'

'He's just stopping in on his way to Sydney. My mum is making me feel so guilty about it, as usual.'

'God, she's such a moll.' Ellie stretched out her vowels on the final word and then flipped the topic back, knowing that Rhiannon never liked to speak about Angela much, 'will Vee come out with us?'

'I doubt it, you know parties aren't really her thing.'

'What is her thing? Besides being an enigma and fucking you.'

'Shut up!' Rhiannon laughed and flicked her wet hands at Ellie, feigning offence. 'You know, she's into movies like we are. But her main thing is the beach.'

'I know, she's a surfer girl without the board. And the tan.'

'Just like you're a horse girl without the…' She paused.

'Careful,' Ellie warned.

'… bad fashion sense.' When Ellie smirked approvingly Rhiannon continued, 'and what am I then?'

'You're a nerd without the social isolation. Duh.'

The next afternoon Rhiannon sat on a bench by the skate park, overlooking the Bellinger. From all around her came the hullabaloo of kids having fun; landing a trick on their boards, leaping from Lavenders

Bridge into the river, discovering a magic mushroom in the cow paddock bordering the park. Beside her, her dad ate quietly and methodically, holding his vegetable pastie at an angle so its contents didn't spill all over him. She had swallowed hers in one gulp, forever a fast eater, and now sat patiently people-watching. She had already exhausted everything she had to say; they had walked around town and her dad had commented on all the trendy boutique stores that were beginning to pop up, he had referred to it as 'gentrification' and explained the meaning when she asked. He hadn't asked about her mother or even herself really; he had that gentle art of allowing someone to open up as and if they wished, just spoke and listened and made you feel comfortable in whatever mode of conversation you took.

When he left, Rhiannon headed to the map in the middle of town, where she had agreed to meet her mum. Angela arrived ahead of time and Rhiannon could sense the mood in the car before she even opened the door, could see it through the windscreen as her mother pulled in, in the tense knuckles on the steering wheel and the way her eyebrows arched above her sunnies. She girded her loins in preparation. 'So, how was he?'

'Um good I guess he –'

'Not that you can trust any answer from him. Or anything he says. Your father –' and she was off on a monologue that began with a stripping down off him, and somehow midway transformed into haranguing Rhiannon. She became steadily more agitated, took her corners with more speed and less concern, anger emanating in chilling waves that froze Rhiannon as they always did. Any demanded answer she gave was monosyllabic, and felt as slow and heavy as the molasses she had slurped the day before.

'So he's got time for you does he? Well he never had time for me, what is it that makes you so special, I know you think you're so smart and you look down on me because I just have *general* knowledge and you've got *specific* knowledge, I know you look down on your own mother, don't try and hide that from me. But you know there's one thing you don't have, and that's friends. And you know why? It's because you're emotionally retarded.' By this point she had begun to sob as she spoke, which shook her shoulders down to the wheel and caused them to careen wildly across the road. 'You're completely incapable of having any emotions or any real connections. And that just makes me so sad. That – I've – given – birth – to a – stunted – daughter... ' each word punctuated with a rasp as she choked for air between her tears. Rhiannon wondered if she could even see past her fogged frames, '... who will always be alone...' She gave a final jerk, perhaps to correct their direction, and the car swerved off the road, along a grass verge and hit a speed sign with a thwonk that cut the engine off. Angela cried for a few more minutes. Rhiannon hardly breathed in that time. Eventually her mother turned on the ignition, reversed away from the pole and declared, her voice back under control, '... You will always be alone, Rhiannon. And that makes me very sad.' Next time her dad suggested they meet up she would say no. It wasn't worth the punishment that followed.

That night Ellie and Rhiannon walked four kilometres to the house party from Ellie's. They both drank as they walked, pausing to scull the goon sack they had split the cost of. By the time they arrived they were very drunk. Rhiannon felt completely self-destructive. Ellie wanted to let loose before they started year eleven in two days' time. 'Legless' was an apt description, considering the way they both seemed to trip over things that weren't there, and the fact that Ellie had even fallen down a cliff in the dark, her fall broken by a roadside lantana bush that was thankfully only two metres down. Rhiannon waved down a ute of young boys who laughingly reached down to pull Ellie out.

'Youse are wasted! Want a lift to Waterfall Way?'

They got chucked out at the top of the road where it met Waterfall Way, giggled their way across the main road and began to make their way down the long, treacherous driveway opposite. They could hear 'Bonkers' playing as they came up to the front door, goon sack swinging half full from Rhiannon's hand as she propped Ellie up with the other. The door was wide open and the room was filled with mainly boys, faces that blurred into each other till Nat called their name from a corner couch she was squished into. They fell into the couch opposite her, limbs akimbo and heads reeling, and Rhiannon closed her eyes to try stop the room from spinning. It didn't help. The conversation was clatter around her, and for a long stretch of time she couldn't decipher any of it at all, till she felt Ellie elbow her ribs.

'She's got one of them hamburger pussies, you can tell,' a guy's voice said with authority. 'Skinny girls have always got fat pussies. Look at the way her legs are spread.'

Rhiannon peeled her eyes open to see a scrawny boy with a shorts tan holding court, gesturing at her and Ellie who both had their legs sprawled, unconsciously flashing their undies at those opposite. The room was silent, whether because people were agreeing with what he said or too shocked to say anything, Rhiannon couldn't tell.

'Stop talking about us,' she slurred.

'I'm not talking about you; I'm talking about the Asian one. With the juicy pussy.'

'You're gross,' Nat said with disdain, crossing the room to the others. 'Come on, guys, let's go outside.' She rolled them a cigarette on the front lawn and spoke to them both, tried her best to pull them together and help them sober up. But as more people showed up to the party and the music got louder they all got separated. Rhiannon kept sucking on the goon as if it were a comforting teat, cradling it in her arms and speaking to it in a hushed voice as if it were her friend.

'Now let's just find some scissors,' she said to the goon sack as she searched through the kitchen drawers. How much time had passed she didn't know. She found the upstairs bathroom and closed the door, lost all her usual cautiousness and began to saw up her inner arm, from elbow to wrist, counting aloud as she did so, one cut for every year of her life. Yes, that sounded good, and it felt good too, though she really had to hack away with those blunt blades.

The door slammed open and Ellie lurched into the room, only just making it to the bathtub before projectile vomiting. She looked up, burped an 'oh, Rhi' when she saw the mess of her arm, and then kept hurling. Nat followed shortly after, assessed the situation in a shrewd glance and quickly locked the door from the inside.

'O-*kay*, let's get the two of youse cleaned up.' She took the scissors, crusted with chop, from Rhiannon's loose hand.

'What were you thinking?' she asked as she rifled through the cabinet above the sink, found some tea tree oil and band aids. She began daubing it on with toilet paper and then meticulously covered each cut. Rhiannon, even through her numbness, buzzed from the gentle maternal gestures, didn't want to move in case it stopped. The blood began to soak the band aids and seep out the sides though, so Nat took off the light jacket she wore. 'Here, put this on. We don't want anyone seeing that.'

'But it'll get stained,' Rhiannon protested, half-heartedly.

'It doesn't matter. Now – ' turning to the sink again she threw the toothbrushes out of the cup, rinsed it efficiently and filled it with water and handed it to Ellie, 'drink this – it'll help.'

Ellie gratefully gulped, gagged and vomited some more till all she was throwing up was bile. She leaned onto the toilet bowl to rest, her cheek pressed against the cool ceramic. Eventually she swished her mouth out with water from the cup and was able to breathe a 'thanks.'

'You're welcome. Youse really made a mess of yourselves, hey. Anyway seems like it's the night for it. Jason and Jacob are having a punch on downstairs and Jason's tooth got knocked out. There's blood. Not as much blood as up here, though... how are you feeling, Rhi? Are you okay? Sober enough to walk?'

'Yeah, I'm fine. Sorry. I can take Ellie home. The night air will probably be good for us.' She was more mortified than drunk now anyway.

Ellie stopped to heave a few times on the walk back, palms on her knees and head held between her legs, splattering the bitumen with bile. Rhiannon pulled her most of the way by hand, the alcohol still in her system giving her extra strength and energy. As she did, Ellie told her about that guy who had talked about her pussy in front of the others.

'He kept following me around. And you know I was so drunk, so I kept sitting down coz I couldn't stand anymore. And then every time I did he'd be next to me, and then his hand was in my dress and then he was fingering me. And I'd kinda moan coz it was awkward and I didn't know what to do, but then I'd be like I don't want this, so I'd get up to go and I'd leave and walk to a different room and sit down there to sober up and he'd follow me and it'd happen again. That happened three times and eventually I just wanted him to leave me alone and to get his hands out of my pants and he kept bugging me, 'Give us a gobby give us a gobby give us a gobby.' He wouldn't shut up and I didn't wanna put my mouth there obviously so to shut him up I gave him a wristy and then he spurted all over my hand and then I knew I was gonna vomit so I got up to go and that's when I came and found you.'

'Yuck, what an idiot. Couldn't he tell you didn't want it?'

'Yeah I mean you'd think so, I can't have been enjoying it that much if I kept walking out half way through. Maybe he didn't though. Or maybe he just didn't care. I don't know.'

By the time they reached hers Ellie had almost sobered up, and as they stepped into the shower together, Rhiannon sliding with relief till she sat at the bottom and open mouthed, began to drink the water as it fell from above, Ellie had turned to care and worry for her friend. She bathed her arm for her and then they sat in the tub as water pooled around them. They sat there till the water was pink tinged and their fingers pruned.

Ellie looked for a bandage while Rhiannon towelled herself down, condemning herself as she did so. 'So stupid, so stupid, why did I do that, I'm such an idiot.'

'It's all good, we can hide it till it heals,' Ellie said reassuringly, as she wound the cotton bandage tightly around her friend's arm.

10

The most exciting thing about starting year eleven at CHEC, which combined a university, TAFE and senior high school all on the one campus, was not having to wear a uniform. Ellie and Rhiannon spent the night before on the phone working out what they would wear to make the best possible impression on their first day. They caught the bus in together. This one took them straight from Bellingen to the school, which was tucked away next to the Coffs Harbour airport, passing through suburbs they weren't familiar with on the way.

'My brother says Toormina High is dodgy as,' Nat said as they stopped opposite it to pick up some people.

'Not as dodgy as that suburb they got rid of,' Rhiannon said.

'What do you mean? How can you get rid of a suburb?'

'It was called Bayldon. They merged it into the two surrounding ones coz it had such a bad rep that people didn't wanna buy property there or whatever.' Ellie looked at her in silence, incredulous.

'Don't look at me like that! I picked up that fact in my time at BDC; what can I say, I'm a Coffs girl now too, babe, I'm not so parochial anymore.'

'Toormy isn't actually that bad.' A girl sitting in the seat in front of them turned round. Her clothes had obviously been chosen to accentuate her features – Daisy Dukes making her tanned muscular legs seem longer, flimsy cotton blouse with the lace of her push up bra visible. She looked familiar to Rhiannon somehow.

'Sorry I couldn't help overhearing. And figured we're going to the same place and probably in the same year so... I'm Esther, Essie.'

They all introduced themselves and Rhiannon realised where she knew her from. Zoe had showed her Esther's Myspace. Esther Jones.

She was one of those girls whose reputations preceded her. She was notorious around Coffs, to the point that she was almost mythological. As are all sluts, really – the only names that carry a bit of bite with them, that hasten up conversations when dropped into them, harry them like a heeler at the heels of a herd, turn the most mundane talk into gossip. 'You guys all from Bello High?'

'Pretty much. You from Toormina?' Rhiannon answered for all of them, being the least suspicious of strangers and also less nervous. It wasn't the first time she'd ventured out of the shire for high school, and she was confident about knowing more people there.

'Jetty. I used to go to Toormina. That's why I was saying it isn't that bad, you know, by comparison. There's a reason it's called Jetty Jail. Anyway, I'm excited for this place. You know there's no punishment system *and* we can smoke on campus?'

'Yeah so good, I guess that's why so many people leave to it. Like we're gonna get treated like adults. Two-hour classes and can call teachers by their first name. It's kinda eliminating that weird hierarchy and also like a transition to self-motivated learning like what you have to do in uni,' said Rhiannon, sounding like a promotional flyer for the new school. As they pulled up to the curb she noticed Vee slouched on a seat out the front of the school and began to wave, forgetting she was behind tinted windows.

'Who's that? She's heaps hot,' Esther asked.

'My girlfriend,' Rhiannon brimmed with pride.

'Girlfriend? Are you, like, lesbo?'

'Yeah,' Rhiannon began to follow Ellie and Nat down the bus aisle, riffling through her leather shoulder bag as she did to check she hadn't left anything, as Esther followed behind her.

'You're pretty hot for a lesbian. I've actually never really talked to one before. Like, I didn't even know there were gay people at our age. Guess I was wrong.' Rhiannon bristled at the comment, but glancing back at her expression all she saw was an unassuming openness and decided Esther didn't know she was being rude. She quickly forgave her for the insensitivity. 'Uh, thanks.'

'Can I ask you something? How do lesbians have sex?' She was too eager to even wait for the go-ahead.

'Wow, straight to the $64,000 question!'

'I like being upfront. I hate when people are just like bla-de-bla-bla-bla and you know they don't care. And neither do you. Besides, you can always say you don't want to answer or like shut up Essie go and Yahoo answers it.'

'True, I could,' Rhiannon said as they stepped off the bus. She held out her hand to the waiting Vee, who was standing with Ellie and Nat, pulled her in for a chaste kiss and then gestured at Esther; 'Vee, this is Essie; Essie, Vee. We just met on the bus.'

'Hey,' Vee said. She gave her hand into Esther's friendly grasp.

'What's with your fingers?' Esther asked, not letting go of her grip and peering down curiously.

Rhiannon was affronted on behalf of Vee, even though Vee seemed completely unbothered, nothing upsetting the smooth surface of serenity and composure that was her most compelling trait. She went to say something but Ellie beat her to it with a valley girl voice – 'Um, Essie, you can't just ask someone why their fingers are webbed!'

'Oh my god, that was so deserved, sorry it just caught my eyes coz I was like rewatching this movie last night that I used to watch as a kid called *The Secret of Roan Inish* – have you guys seen it? – and the woman in it is like this seal woman and has fingers like yours.'

Vee snatched her hand back out of Esther's with a suddenness that surprised them all. Her unusually big irises showed a flash of white around them, something Ellie instinctively recognised as fear, used to reading it in her horses. She glanced at Rhiannon to see if she noticed it too, and saw she was frowning slightly, perturbed.

Rhiannon commandeered a huge table for them to all sit at for lunch, right in the centre of the quadrangle, partially shaded from the summer glare by an acacia. With Ellie, Nat, Zoe, Vee, Keira and Cam they made a flock of feminine energy that drew people towards them – or at least it drew Esther in again. She seemed determined to solidify herself in the friend group; who knew what toxic slut shaming she wanted to leave behind her? They all lay their legs out in the sun to tan, took turns ordering at the cafeteria, checked out the university students that milled around the library. Sparrows hopped beneath the tables picking at scattered crumbs, and spindly-legged ibis stalked through the quad, poking their protuberant beaks into the bins. Rhiannon realised she was made distinctly cooler than she was at Bishop, with the addition of more established 'hot girls' like Ellie, Nat and Esther. What was it about social status in high school that your own glory relied so heavily on who you mixed with? Just like that group of boys with surfer tans and floppy hair one table over that Nat kept eyeing off, known by their group name and group prowess.

'Who are they?' Nat asked.

'They're the K crew. For Korora. Don't even bother with them,' Zoe answered.

'They've got such huge egos,' Rhiannon added.

'I mean I get it though, some of them are soooo hot,' Nat said. She gazed at them longingly.

'I meant it when I said don't bother with them. They have a list of rules for girls they can date. They're dicks.'

'Wait what do you mean?'

'They have a literal list. It got sent round last year. No fat girls, no girls with big noses, no girls with moles, no sluts and so on,' Zoe explained, shaking her head with disdain as she did.

'Oh. Well, that defs cancels me out then,' Nat said, and gestured at her prominent nose and the mole above her upper lip.

'I love your beauty spot.' Ellie came round behind her and hugged her from the back, and Nat leaned back into the hug.

One of the boys, delighted by the physical contact, yelled out as he walked past; 'Oh yeah, lesbians! Go for it.'

'Wow. What an idiot,' Rhiannon said.

'I guess word's gotten round about you guys. You're definitely the only like out couple in the whole school and the blood's gone to their dicks now so they've got even less in their brains and are even more stupid than normal. Do you guys wanna know a really funny story?' Esther hardly gave time for them to answer before ploughing onwards, 'One time I was in a bed with two of them after a party, one on each side, and, like, they both wanted to get with me and started to try feel me up and they misjudged where I was and were actually feeling each other up.'

'Oh. My. God. That's like the funniest thing I've ever heard,' Zoe gasped as she wiped tears from her eyes.

'And quite hot too to be honest...' Cam let the sentence hang. It was the closest he'd come to announcing his own sexuality. Rhiannon kindly picked it up for him so he didn't regret exposing himself, agreeing it would be hot if they actually got together.

'What does Flynn think of them?' Ellie asked Keira.

'Oh, he thinks they're idiots. Too conceited. They look up to him though coz he's a good surfer.'

'They'll probably be nice to you by extension,' Ellie added.

'Great, I look forward to it.' Keira rolled her eyes and the others grinned.

Through all the banter Rhiannon noticed that Vee was zoned out, looking out across the pebbled quad towards the seagulls that fought each other for discarded chips on the lunch tables, the only one not engaging in any of their back and forth, her expression seemingly mimicking the twists and turns of the gulls' arguments. She smiled when a puny one finally secured a chip, frowned when an ibis came along and broke up the disturbance, sending the gulls wheeling off into the sky, back to their ocean home. Did she wish she was free to leave too, to bicker with mutton birds near their burrowed nests, to rest with wings spread in warm upward currents of air, to have saltwater slide off waterproof feathers, to be impervious to weather, unaffected by society dictated timetables and timelines?

That night Rhiannon went back to Vee's. She had the go ahead from her mum, who was less concerned with her staying over at a friend's house on a weeknight when it was the beginning of term. She was subdued as Vee drove them back to Urunga, unsure how to broach the topic she so desperately wanted to. Vee's dad was out, so she made tacos for her mum and Rhi, encouraging her mum to sit at the dining room table with them in a way Rhiannon could tell wasn't the norm. Isla spoke to her more than she had on previous occasions, perhaps because she had come over enough that she recognised Rhiannon as a 'special friend,' which is how she referred to her.

'Do you swim, Rhiannon?' The whole household seemed to revolve around the ocean and its moods, maybe the only thing that tied them together. Certainly the only conversation Rhiannon ever saw Vee and her dad engage in was in regards to the surf.

'Ahh yeah I mean, I love the river near mine. But I'm not a swimmer like Vee.'

'Aye, oor Vee, she's a wonderful swimmer, that she is.'

'Do you swim much?' Rhiannon could tell she'd erred in the way Vee tensed up next to her.

'She doesn't like to swim here,' Vee interjected and, swiftly changing topics, 'we have such a huge year at this new school Mither! Two hundred and fifty kids in year eleven alone.'

But her mother was not to be deterred. Placing her hand over Rhiannon's she commanded her attention and eye contact, and Rhiannon noticed she had the same strange eyes as Vee – with irises so dark and pupils so large that they seemed to fill her entire eyeball, not even a flicker of white to rim the edges.

'The water is too warm here. And hid's too lonely. I dinnae understand their voices, or their currents. And I cannae swim far, not in this skin. Not with these feet!' And she kicked her feet out from under the table in disgust.

Rhiannon side-eyed Vee, wanted to take her hand out from underneath Isla's but was scared of escalating the situation. She was obviously so drunk, and drunk people were best to be humoured, especially when they talked nonsense. Vee tried again, and failed, to swing the conversation round to school. Isla just lent more weight on Rhiannon's hand, pinning her to the table, her whisky breath making Rhiannon shut her mouth and breathe through her nose to escape it.

'I miss wur sleek bodies together. And I miss the baskin' and the howlin' and the pups in their coats of fluff. Vee knows I love her but hid's no the same. I have tae go hame. Help me go hame.'

It was a direct appeal, said with such sincerity and pity, that Rhiannon was confronted. What could she possibly say? She was clearly mentally unhinged, and Vee was already mortified, trying to hush her mum, she didn't want to embarrass her further.

She settled on 'I'm sorry,' and she meant it. She was sorry for Vee, sorry for Isla, sorry she couldn't ease her pain in any way. After they washed up Vee lingered around the living room, ensuring Isla was comfortable and dozing before she let Rhiannon lead the way to the bedroom.

'What was she talking about?' She wasn't expecting any answer, least of all the one she got.

Afterwards, her head reeling, she repeated the bare bones back to Vee, trying to shape it into a semblance of something she could grapple with, thinking if she repeated it enough times it would sink in. Vee's mother was a selkie, a seal woman. But Vee wasn't one, just had some of the attributes, and that's why her hands were that way. Her father had met her years ago, on a beach in Orkney, and had taken her sealskin so that she couldn't change back and leave him. It sounded completely absurd, yet it somehow made sense, or it at least made sense of so many of the strange things she had noticed about Vee. Her proclivity for the ocean, the way Ajax responded to her, her uncanny calm, even her scent.

'Yes. And Rhi,' Vee grabbed her hands tight just like her mother had done, 'you have to help me help her.'

'Help her what?'

'Escape.'

11

The first five weeks of CHEC Rhiannon struggled to dress for the weather while also hiding her slowly healing scars. It was still hot, Australia's summer a seemingly unending one that reaches from October to March. She was usually more sensible about where she cut once the weather warmed up, choosing the hideaway close to her armpit, but in her drunkenness she had thought of nothing but the immediate easing of her turmoil. She got into the habit of wearing a jumper, that she would take off and leave only on her left arm, as if to carry it more casually, and when she did have it off completely she spoke at all times with her left wrist held tight across her torso, holding on to her right forearm as her right hand did all the gesticulating on its own.

She settled into a routine. Catching the bus in with Ellie and the other girls, fucking Vee in the back of her car in free periods, coming home to the green tree frogs squatting in the toilet bowl as they always did, flushed down only to crawl back out and croak in the echoing porcelain once again. Vee's revelation slowly permeated into her consciousness, till it was as real as the seat buckle digging into her back mid-screw, something she accepted as 'just is.' Having been raised on children's books influenced by Celtic mythology, consuming *The Chronicles of Prydain* alongside *Harry Potter*, she had been primed for such a reveal. And there was no reason not to believe her first love; she trusted her with her heart and her hands inside her, so why not this?

She had no idea how to help her though, and Vee hadn't raised it again, had retreated into her usual concealedness. Rhiannon thought about telling Ellie, but thought her having not interacted with Isla or having seen the bizarreness of her first hand, it would all seem too farfetched. So she let it sit. As they sat on the school bus on the way home it felt like it was between them though, the only secret she'd ever kept hidden from her. Ellie knew the origin of every scar she hid away on the soft parts of her skin, even ones that Vee didn't, she stored some of her memories for her like all old friends do, remembering things that you've forgotten yourself. It was a rowdy bus trip that day; a few Bello boys they knew who had spent the day in Coffs were on it, one tipsy and raucous and the other stoned and slumped in the corner of the back seat. The obnoxious one began rating the girls, loudly giving Nat a 2/10 much to her chagrin and without her asking, till Esther turned on him and told him to get fucked, said he wasn't one to talk, he couldn't get a root in a brothel.

'Rhi, look!' Ellie poked her in the ribs and pointed at the blazed boy; out of the backpack on his lap came a puppy's head, tan and panting.

'Jacob, what the hell! Have you got a dog in your bag?!'

'Shhhh, the bus driver'll kick me off. I had to hide her in here.'

'She's so cute! Can you get her out so we can see her?'

He pulled her out and they rubbed her vigorously, noticing as they did so that she had dicks drawn in permanent marker all over her short Staffy scruff. 'What's her name?' Rhiannon asked.

'Haven't named her yet. I only got her today. My mate owed me for bud so he paid me in a pup.'

'Oh my god that's such a good trade,' Ellie squealed as the puppy licked her hands.

'Yeah except my mum's gonna kill me, hey. She says we've already got enough. Except one of ours died a few weeks back and I swear the other one hasn't wagged its tail since.'

'Awwww,' they cooed. Not just over the puppy but also from seeing Jacob so sedate. Last time they'd come across him he was drinking straight whisky under a fig tree at 9am, and called them a bunch of sluts. It was a nice change.

They played with her the rest of the way, even sat with him for ten minutes at the bus stop once they got into town, till Sasha dragged Ellie off to IGA to help her with the groceries.

'How are you getting home?' Jacob asked Rhiannon.

'My mum's picking me up,' she said curtly. Five minutes later, her mum still wasn't there, and so she called her on reverse charges. Angela picked up immediately. 'Hey, I was just wondering how far off you are?'

'I don't know, maybe four hours, maybe more.'

'Wait, what?'

'I'm in Coffs Harbour, about to go to the movies and then have dinner with Diane. Her husband has just left her for a younger woman, a *receptionist*, and she needs the company,' she pronounced the profession as if it were a profanity.

'Wait how will I get home, though? The Thora bus has gone.'

'That's not my problem, you can call up your father, you're his responsibility too. He can sort it out for once.'

'He lives in Queensland...'

'So? You're his daughter.'

'Okay... I don't have any money on me to get dinner while I wait. My Centrelink doesn't come in till Friday.'

'That's not my problem. I'm having the evening off, spending time the way I want to for once. Call your father.' She hung up.

Rhiannon stared down at her mobile in shock. She felt sick. Should she walk the fifteen kilometres home? There were so many trucks on the road, though. It was too scary. She could walk to Nat's, she supposed, but they weren't close enough friends to just invite herself over for dinner with her family or tell her that her mum had left her. She could call Vee but it would take her ages to get there... and besides, she didn't want to tell her. It was another thing she kept hidden from her. She didn't want anyone to know what had just happened, didn't want people to figure out that she was alone at the bus stop as the sun went down and the night grew colder. The only person she would be okay with knowing was Ellie... Ellie – maybe she was still here!

She power walked to IGA, not even giving a second glance to a goat tied out the front, and paced the aisles, the knot in her stomach tightening as she found each one empty. But then she got to the deli. There, to her instant relief, was Sasha. She sidled up slowly and shyly.

Sasha turned. 'You looking for Ellie? She's just at the butchers' grabbing sausages.'

'Yeah. Um. Sasha. Could I maybe get a lift home? I know it's out of your way.'

'Where's your mother?' she looked at her sharply.

'She's in Coffs seeing a movie with a friend.' Rhiannon was terrified of having to say more than that, felt nauseated with having exposed anything, there was something deeply wrong with her as a daughter to be in this situation, to have to ask.

'Sure,' Sasha saved her from giving an explanation by adding, 'how about you go round up Ellie for me, and I'll meet you at the car, it's parked just out the front.' Rhiannon skittered off gratefully.

That weekend Ellie invited Esther over to hang with her and Rhiannon. The three of them had bonded fast, aided by Esther's gregariousness. Sasha left them to their own devices and went into Coffs for a work function and Vee came by in the late afternoon, picking up pizzas in town on her way. The four of them lazed around the living room, sipping on Smirnoff double blacks that made them feel very sophisticated, playing 'never have I ever' half-heartedly as Esther regaled them with her slutty escapades. She was a true storyteller, able to draw out tension and build it to a climax. Rhiannon had never really appreciated it as an art form before, but now that she saw it done skilfully she realised how frustrated she was by people that butchered a good story, and also how oral storytelling was such an important part of so many cultures.

At dusk Ellie announced she had to feed the horses, and the others decided to come along, finding joy in the feed room just as Rhiannon did. The horses were waiting at the gate already, Gemma pawing at it in impatience so that her hoof caught on the bottom rung and the gate jolted on its hinges, loudly clanging and declaring her desire for dinner. Ludo, lower in the hierarchy, stood further back, waiting patiently with a willy wagtail atop his withers, its fan tail twitching from side to side, bird shit in white streaks on his coat beneath it. A cream bird with a pale, yellow bill stalked elegantly further back, in expectation of the grain discards too small for the horses' lips to mouth up.

'What bird is that?' Esther asked.

'An egret – beautiful isn't it?' Rhiannon answered as she opened the gate for Ellie, whose hands were full with the buckets.

'That would make a sick baby name, for a girl.'

They began to discuss dream names as the horses plunged nose deep into their feed, Gemma whisking her tail and firing a warning shot with her right hind every few minutes. Ellie stood with her back leaning slightly on the mare's shoulder as Esther and Rhiannon each sat on a gate post. The sound of the horses' eating was calming, and in the encroaching darkness they didn't notice Vee had climbed the fence and wandered off till they heard a low 'fuck!'

'Are you okay?' Rhiannon jumped off the post, landing unsteadily on her tipsy feet.

'Something's stung me, this plant.'

'Did you grab at the elephant ears? They're down in that damp corner, people always go for them. We'll put some aloe vera on it back at the house,' Ellie was unbothered, didn't move from her spot with the mare as back support.

'No, it's this stuff at my ankles.'

'Oh, you went into the stinging nettle patch! All good, we'll find you some dock leaves, they always grow nearby. Essie, you wanna come help?' Rhiannon called over her shoulder, as she set about searching the grey ground for the low-lying plant. Eventually she found some and instructed Vee to stay still while she rubbed the leaves over her shins, which had raised pink dots all over them.

'Does that really work?' Esther sounded doubtful.

'Course it does, natural remedy!' Rhiannon rubbed all the more vigorously till the leaves began to crumble in her hands.

'What did you call what stung me again – a nettle of some kind?'

'Stinging nettle.'

'I think they're on Orkney too; my mum has spoken about them.'

'Yeah, that makes sense, they're an introduced species here, the Brits brought them over. And supposedly they were brought there by the Romans, so really we've got them to blame.'

'Well I'll never ask what the Romans have ever done for us again...' Ellie's voice carried out of the half-dark and Rhiannon and Vee both laughed at the Monty Python reference.

'Why were you all the way over here anyway?' Rhiannon asked Vee.

'I didn't wanna spook the horses by getting too close.'

'They're fine with strangers – look at Essie now –' Ellie gestured at Ludo, and sure enough Esther had her arms wrapped around his thick neck as he ate and he paid less attention to her than if she were a fly, 'and besides, you've met them before anyway.'

As Rhiannon and Vee came closer though, Gemma stopped eating, raised her head with ears pricked and pushed her top lip back till her gums and row of yellowing teeth were visible.

'Why's she doing that?' Esther asked. 'She looks like a giraffe.'

'I don't know. It's called the flehmen response. It means she's smelt something strange; I don't know what she could have smelt, though.' As Ellie said this Gemma blew out of her nostrils, hard, and took a sudden step sideways, shying away from Rhiannon and Vee. Ellie immediately lost her balance and fell on her arse in the dust, and Esther began to cackle. She soon noticed that the others weren't laughing though, they all seemed abnormally serious and were dodging each other's glances. As Ellie got to her feet, brushing the dirt off her shorts, there was a perplexed frown on her face as she looked at Rhiannon, as if trying to understand something; and Rhiannon in turn was looking at Vee, trying to catch her eye. Vee ignored them both and walked quickly to the fence line and vaulted over using a fence post and the bottom strand as a push off.

'We going back up then?' Esther asked, semi rhetorically, thrown off by the odd behaviour of the three girls.

'Yep, it's pretty much dark, let's go,' and Ellie held the gate open for her, just a shape in the deep, deep twilight.

Back inside, they ate some more pizza, had a shot each and their moods began to lift again. Esther suggested they play a card game, but Rhiannon vehemently opposed it, 'I hate card games.'

'Really?!'

'She hates board games too. Anything competitive stresses her out,' Ellie said.

'What, why?'

Rhiannon seemed reluctant to answer, and then gave a rushed sentence, 'oh my mum has just always been really competitive and growing up those things weren't fun to play, they always turned into something else.'

'True, fair enough,' Esther said.

Later on, as they lay with their arms wrapped around each other in the spare bedroom, Rhiannon tentatively asked Vee why she had been afraid of the horses' reactions. 'Because I'd come straight from my mum. They'd be able to smell her on me. It's not a normal smell for a horse.'

Emboldened by her own frankness, Vee then asked Rhiannon what else, like card games, she didn't like. Rhiannon hesitated.

'You don't have to answer if you don't want to.'

'No, I'm just thinking about it,' but really she was mustering up the right tone. 'Well, I guess, birthdays and presents are another one that most other people like.'

'Birthdays I get, people place so much unnecessary expectation and emphasis on them. Makes them more stress than they're worth.'

'Totally! And like I find it so weird being congratulated on something I didn't achieve – being born on a particular day?! So weird. Or are people being like 'well done for surviving that long'?'

'What about presents?'

'I just think they're so often given as a show, more for the other person than for you. And they're manipulative. Like a bribe. You know, 'now I've given you this, you have to give me that in return or do this or be that kind of person.' They always have a catch.'

'I'm sorry that's how she's used them with you,' Vee said as she kissed her on the forehead, pulling her more tightly against her. From the other room they could hear Ellie and Esther choking on giggles. It made the room feel bigger, and Rhiannon even smaller, but not quite small enough for what she wanted. She wriggled herself back into Vee, wishing she could be encased by her, live inside her, and never go home.

12

'Come over to mine after school Friday night. Let's have a party to celebrate the end of term one,' Ellie passed the message to Keira in English at the tail end of March, adding by way of explanation, 'My mum'll be there but she's so chill, she'll let us have the upstairs to ourselves.'

'Who's coming?'

'Well, I've invited Zoe, Cam, Rhi, Vee, Essie, Nat, Nat's brother will probably come, you can bring Flynn too, obviously, and some of my friends at Bello High that you may not know. There'll probably be like ten or fifteen of us so not huge coz I don't wanna make it too chaotic for Sasha, but it'll be fun.'

'Who's Sasha?'

'Oh, my mum, sorry. I call her by her name sometimes.'

'Sick, yeah me and Flynn will come then.'

In the quad afterwards Zoe interrogated Ellie on her invitees. 'You didn't ask any of the K crew did you?'

'Of course not, duh.'

'They'd want to be invited, though,' Rhiannon said. 'Do you know what one of them said to me the other day? "Get me some of that Bello punani, especially Ellie's, hers is the finest."'

'Yuck,' Ellie was both affronted and flattered, but she crossed her brown legs beneath her short skirt, suddenly self-conscious of what lay between them. Smoothing her hands down her thighs she glanced across at their table, where a few of them slouched in beanies, keeping their heads warm post autumn morning surf.

'Is Vee actually gonna come? She doesn't usually like to get loose does she?' Zoe turned on Rhiannon, fixing her with a gaze that demanded an answer and hinted that she knew there was more to it that she was determined to find out.

'Lots of people don't like to get loose,' Keira defended the absent Vee, and Rhiannon smiled at her in thanks before stating, unequivocally, that yes, she would be there.

Friday night rolled around, and Vee found herself unusually wasted. Zoe was right that she didn't like to get loose, didn't like to lose control, was scared of what secrets could come spilling out. The house had filled quickly, and it was in one of those rare moments of clarity stuffed in among a whole succession of drunken escapades that she came to, sprawled against a sofa later in the night. A boy sat next to her, and someone's legs were thrust out over her shoulder. She felt around the ankle and then, unable to recognise the person from the shape of the bone, gave a tug and demanded to know who was draped all over her.

'It's Marley,' said the boy next to her, not taking his eyes from the cigarette he was struggling to roll.

'Oh hey, that's for me isn't it?'

'For both of us. Nothing like a durry when you're drunk. Pass that up to Marley would you,' and he indicated the pouch in his lap.

Vee gave the protruding ankle another yank, and a face appeared next to her own, as if it were an old-fashioned bell pull that caused an instant reaction. As Vee leaned back to take in the face that loomed so close to her own, realising that 'Marley' was in fact a girl, not a boy as she had assumed from the name, she suffered an unpleasant spin, her vision reeling. Reaching for the tobacco, the fringed girl thanked her by name, confusing Vee still further.

'Do I know her?' She asked the boy next to her.

'Yeah, I introduced you to her before, you're pretty fucked mind you so you probably don't remember.' He lit the cigarette and passed it to her after a drag, apologising for the slight wet he had left on the end.

'What's your name again?'

'Harry, I've told you at least five times already. I'm Nat's brother.' Vee gave a deliberate ash of the cigarette and refrained from making a sassy reply. Where was Rhi? She hadn't seen her for a while and she had important things to tell her. It was really very necessary that she made her feelings clear, she needed Rhi to understand how much she loved her. On the couch above her she could hear Cam proclaiming to someone loudly, 'I'd always wanted to talk to you at school but I was too scared! You're just so cool and like intimidating.' And it wasn't till he said, 'When you started dating Rhi...' that she realised he was speaking to her. She ignored him and staggered to her feet, muttering a quick apology to the boy beside her, whose name she could not recall. She felt that really, now was the time to declare her undying affection for Rhi, now that vodka had corroded any inhibitions, she could see the path clear ahead of her. After interrupting people hooking up in the spare bedroom she came across Ellie, Nat, Rhiannon and Zoe on Ellie's bed, dresses all hitched around their thighs; all Vee could discern was a messy array of tangled body parts as they rolled around. At first Vee thought it was another sexual scene that she had walked in on but then she heard the giggles as they clutched on to each other, Rhiannon's laughter straining her dress around her waist with each mighty intake of breath.

'Oh hey Vee, can you think of anything that like explodes and floats away in books and movies?'

'Um, what?'

'Well you know like how Aunt Marge in *Harry Potter* gets really big and then floats away? Like expands? We're thinking of other things that do that, we've got six.'

'Like the snake balloon in *Shrek*,' said Ellie.

'What? Isn't it a toad?' Vee asked.

'No, he makes two, a toad and a snake,' Rhiannon said.

'And then me and Rhi read this fantasy book where this guy inflates and floats away –'

'Yeah the slaughterer in the *Sky Pirates* series!' said Rhiannon, bouncing on the bed in her excitement.

'And the puffer fish in *Finding Nemo* and Violet from *Willy Wonka*,' Nat added.

'How are you even thinking of all these? They are so obscure,' Vee lay herself across the spare side of the bed.

'Our brains are just on it, like we're on the same page and when you think about it there are so many! It's like a forgotten trope of movies!' Rhiannon's voice rose to a pitch so excited it was almost a squeal.

'It's just the mushies,' said Zoe and Vee turned to look at her properly for the first time. Bigger than the others, she had breasts that seemed to be expanding by the minute. Her dress was far too tight for her ample chest. It appeared that Rhiannon too had noticed this, for she pointed and said, 'Look, another thing that's exploding and's just about to float away!'

All four began to laugh till they cried and Vee could only sit there with a slightly bemused expression on her face till a Ziploc bag was thrust into it, containing some dingy dried mushrooms.

'I've never had mushrooms before...' she deliberately didn't use 'shrooms' or 'mushies' to intimate her total ignorance of them, and Nat took pity on her.

'You don't have to have any, or just have one or two if you want, then it won't be that strong. Here, roll it up,' she grabbed one and began to smoosh it between her fingers in demonstration, 'and swallow it like a pill. Then it doesn't taste so bad.' As she swallowed the mushroom her face contorted as if she had experienced something truly unpleasant though, and Vee was slightly disconcerted.

'That doesn't work at all, just chew it up. It tastes gross but meh,' shrugged Zoe.

'And actually, Zoe I've just wanted to say this all night, your boobs are amazing. Like I'm straight,' Ellie scanned the room at this, as if waiting for someone to jump out and contradict her, 'but I just want to squeeze them.'

'I agree, I haven't been able to take my eyes off them all night,' Rhiannon said.

'It's just the dress...'

'Me thinks the lady doth protest too much,' said Rhiannon.

'Stop channelling *Hamlet* you creep, you've been doing it all night!' Ellie cried and Vee eagerly participated in the pillow fight that followed. When they all stopped, breathless, they began pleading with Zoe to show them her tits. When she laughingly refused, Vee, who by now felt quite comfortable with them all, as if she were on the inside of whatever collective mania was occurring, said reassuringly, 'Look, you don't have to even show us both. Just show us one and we'll put it next to the mirror and then we'll have two anyway.'

'That is the worst logic I have ever heard,' Nat said, deadpan.

'And you're the one not on mushies!' Laughed Ellie.

Esther arrived, affording everyone a distraction – smiling stupidly, dishevelled and wearing nothing but cotton undies and Ray-Bans. With the hyper-consciousness of a lesbian paranoid to be perceived as a predator, Vee carefully averted her gaze from the brazen public nudity so as not to be seen to be paying unnecessary attention to the bare breasts before her. The others seemed completely unconcerned as Esther plonked herself on the bed and began to use one arm of her sunnies to twitch them up and down, grinning about her in what she obviously thought was a very winning way.

'Put some clothes on Essie,' Ellie said, though it was apparent from her tone that she really didn't care either way and was only saying it out of a sense of propriety.

'I *am* wearing clothes,' and Esther tweaked the Ray-Bans up and down again enthusiastically, as if to say 'exhibit A!'

Then Vee felt herself looking at Esther and all the others on the bed with her and noticing, as if for the first time, how very attractive they all were. The pleasant tingling she got as she shuffled closer to Rhiannon, her bare calves within reach of her hand, grew to a self-incriminating wetness in her underwear. She looked at Rhiannon and Rhiannon looked back at her, mouthing 'let's go' and Vee grinned and nodded. They exited the bedroom without drawing much attention, the others distracted by Esther, who was on one, ranting about someone – who, Vee didn't care. But she could hear her voice still on the stairs, entering her ears as she entered Rhiannon, who snatched the hem of her dress out of the way so Vee could finger fuck her in the stairwell.

'Oh I don't know, she might be gay, I don't really care either way. It's just funny coz she's so intent on proving it. It's all over her Tumblr. I just feel like each time she came up for air during her muff dive she would breathe, "I am, I am, I am." For her, sleeping with people is a statement of who she is. Anyway, enough about her, let me tell you what I have to tell you. Guess who I just fucked in the other room.'

'Wait, you had sex in my spare room?!' Ellie said in faux outrage.

'Yes I did, but I'm not the only guilty one. I walked in on Flynn and Keira making out and the-*en...*' she extended the word to draw out suspense and the rest of the room went up in shrieks of, 'Oh my god, tell us!'

'They're too loud, can we go further away, do you think?' Vee whispered in Rhiannon's ear, and Rhiannon grabbed her hand and yanked her along the hallway to the downstairs bathroom and shut them in. She tugged her underwear off and hopped up on to the sink in one move, legs spread and labia glistening so all Vee could think of was tonguing her clit. As they went at it a knock came at the door and a voice said, 'Can I come in? I think I'm gonna be sick.'

Zoe barrelled in, fell on her knees at the tub as if in worship and began to heave. Rhiannon leapt down to her aid. 'Get it all out, it's just the shrooms. They make me nauseous too... once this passes you'll be fine.'

As she vomited, there was the sound of a knock again and the girls looked up to see Sasha standing in the open doorway, holding a glass. Her curly hair was mussed up as if she'd just risen from sleep and they sheepishly remembered that this was the reason Ellie had told them all not to carry the party downstairs, because it might disturb Sasha as her bedroom was on that level.

'Here, Rhi, give her this when she's finished. It's soda water with Hydralyte. It'll help settle her stomach. When you're done, can you move to the bathroom upstairs? You're waking me up down here.'

Vee blushed and Rhiannon apologised, both conscious of their clumsy initiation of fucking, and worried it was that that had roused her. As she walked off, Zoe stared intently at the gap in the doorway in which she had stood.

'Who was that?' she asked, almost aggressively.

'Ellie's mum.'

'I've seen her at 19 O.'

There was a moment of silence, then Rhiannon said without conviction, 'You can't have.'

'I promise you, it's her. I've seen her there many times.'

'You're tripping. Literally,' Vee was firm.

But Zoe just looked at Rhiannon, till Rhiannon said, 'Don't tell Ellie now. Please.'

A few days later Ellie and Rhiannon sat at their favourite meeting spot, Summervilles Bridge, both subdued in jeans on the rocks of the riverbank. It was already too icy to splash in the shallows in the Easter holidays; the Rosewood River flowed straight from the mountains, had a bite to it that the Bellinger only got in winter.

'She said she's wanted to tell me for ages. And like it's what's got us this house here, and pays for my horses. She said she's only done it for us... but how can she say something so shameful has been done because of and for me? I would never ask her or want her to do this... it's disgusting. She could've done anything else. Why this? And to find out this way... I can't trust Zoe not to repeat it.'

'Just deny it if people bring it up. But not in like an insistent way. Or deflect it with a joke. Be like, 'You *wish* your mum was hot enough to be a hooker.' Honestly though I don't know if she will repeat it generally, she didn't seem gossipy about it when I spoke to her. She was more shocked by it, and sad for you.'

'Just as long as she doesn't tell Cam...'

'No one believes what Cam says anyway. He's such a stirrer. It's maybe even better if it comes out via him, it'll immediately discredit it.'

For a few minutes all that could be heard was the babble of the river and the song of the crickets, dispersed with the calls of rainforest birds, till Ellie picked up a large rock and after throwing it from palm to palm she chucked it into the water, creating a disharmonious *plonk*.

'She said she's not ashamed of it Rhini, but I don't know how she couldn't be... it's the worst thing imaginable. And now all I can think about is my father. What if he wasn't a one-night stand? What if he was, you know...'

'There's no point thinking about that, what difference does it make, he's not in your life anyway.'

'Yeah, true. But also it means I come from, like, the seediest possible thing.'

'So what? That doesn't mean anything, it's no reflection on how your life ends up. Sasha is the best. Like I come from a 'legitimate marriage' or whatever and you know what my mum is like. Or look at Vee... her parents are still together and supposedly that's meant to be the best thing for a child, and it looks alright from the outside, like her dad is a successful lawyer or whatever but actually it's... well it's...'

'It's what?'

'Okay, I'm gonna tell you something but you gotta promise not to tell anyone.'

Ellie raised her eyebrows. 'You know I don't repeat anything you tell me.'

'Yeah I know I know, I just had to say coz it's Vee's secret not mine. But actually, now I think about it, maybe bringing you in will be good, I'll tell her I told you. You're like my sister. And maybe you'll be able to help.'

'Okay, now you've got me freaking out. What is it?'

'It's kinda hard to explain, I don't really know where to start but I guess I'll just dive in... so – ' and Rhiannon flicked her hair out of her face and readjusted her legs, settling herself in for a substantial story.

Five minutes later, if you stood on the other side of the riverbank, you would've heard an almost victorious 'I *knew* there was something you guys were keeping from me!' echo across the water.

13

It was a week into the school holidays and Ellie, Rhiannon and Vee lay topless on the yellow sand of Third Headland, coloured by the sandstone of the East coast. Rhiannon had heard that the west coast had white sand because it came from limestone, and she had heard Isla speak of the pebbled beaches of Scotland but she couldn't envision either of them, the beach to her was always soft, bright and embracing. This was an isolated beach, even in the peak of summer, never attracting the tourists of Sawtell or the Promised Lands, and on this autumnal day they had it entirely to themselves. The water was still warm, unlike the rivers of the valley, and they had happily exhausted themselves body surfing and struggling against the undertow, Vee guiding them knowledgeably away from the ever-present rip that the locals knew about, as the beach wasn't patrolled by lifeguards, only accessible by a dirt road full of potholes that crossed the train tracks.

'A beach on the wrong side of the tracks, hey,' Ellie had said as they waited at the boom gate, and after the train passed, they pulled over to play barefoot on the iron railings, seeing who could run the fastest along them without losing their balance.

'Have you ever seen that man in Coffs with the scars all over him from train surfing?' Rhiannon asked Vee.

'No, what happened? What's train surfing?'

'Exactly what it sounds like – when you stand on the roof of a train as it's moving. He got tangled in some electrical wires when he was doing it years and years ago and got third degree burns from it.'

They were all excitable, sprinted across the sand once they parked at the headland, laughed as the wind whipped their hair round their faces and launched themselves into the waves. Now they lay like tired puppies, lulled by the limbo of the afternoon and the holidays. Perhaps the lull had an almost hypnotic effect on Vee, soothing her into an unusual state of security and disclosure, as she began to speak about her family freely, as if to prepare Ellie for meeting them for the first time.

'I've always been so terrified to tell anyone. Growing up my dad drummed it into me that if I told anyone I would lose her forever, because she would be put in a circus or taken away by scientists to be studied. He'd be like, 'You can't do that to her,' and I guess the fear kept me silent. But now I see my silence is slowly killing her... she can't stay here. She's drinking herself to death, seriously. She's always breaking her ribs from falling over and last winter she burnt her ear twice when she passed out on the fire. Let alone whatever it's doing to her mind, being held against her will.'

'So, what happens if you get her 'sealskin' back? She changes back? And goes back? Can she even get back?' Rhiannon was glad Ellie asked. She was too entranced to speak, had never heard Vee talk so openly and was hesitant to probe, hating when people pried into her private life with questions so always reluctant to do the same to others.

'Yeah, she changes back. And I guess she'll try to go back... I don't know if she can, it's so far and not waters she knows. He took her deliberately far away from Orkney to disorientate her, the cunt. But I know she will try. It's all she wishes for.' 'Does that mean you may never see her again?'

'Yeah, I guess it does. I try not to think about that. But like if it comes down to her living in misery here till she dies or having a chance at happiness again without me, I'll take that chance. She's in the wrong shape you see. Selkies are only ever meant to be human for short periods, it's not natural for them to live like she has, as a human for almost two decades.'

Rhiannon thought of *The Last Unicorn*, and how distressed she was when she was turned into a human, how she felt her body dying around her with every second, how she was disoriented by the emotions that came with it, such as regret. Isla said she regretted meeting Vee's father – was that something that only came with being human? Or was it because that when she was in human form that she made, inevitably, human mistakes? Was she scared of forgetting who she was the longer she stayed in this body, just as the unicorn was? Was she driven by the same despair?

'Are there others like her, trapped?'

'Back in her home, yes. She told me she's even heard of harems of selkies, if you can call them that, presided over by one man like a cult, not allowing them to leave. They were nightmare stories told to them growing up, to discourage them from shedding their skin on shore too often, but she said there's truth to them.'

'Wow, like a sex cult of women.'

'Yeah, I guess you could call it that,' Vee's face darkened, 'anyway, we have to do something.'

'We'll work it out, I'm sure we can, can't we, Rhini?'

Rhiannon could only nod in pretend hope, her face not showing the hopelessness she actually felt. The afternoon passed, their skin heated up and eventually their stomachs began to grumble, hunger calling them to Vee's house. They decided to leave and, as they walked towards the dirt track that served as a car park, towels dragging in the dust lazily, they ran into Flynn. Vee stood back as Ellie and Rhiannon chatted to him. 'What's Keira up to? She should come to Bello later on, we're going out,' Ellie said.

'She can't, she's got soccer practice tonight.'

'She plays soccer?!'

'Yeah, in the Orara side, under eighteens.'

'That's hot.' Rhiannon was impressed and inspired, she momentarily wished she were a soccer player, booted and sweaty and shoving against other women's bodies. Did they all switch shirts at the end of a match? Did they run around in tank tops and shorts on a winter evening at training, nipples erect? Did they help each other stretch, thigh muscles taut and a prickle of hair poking out the top of a shin pad?

'Rhi's frothing it. *Bend It Like Beckham* was one of our favourite movies growing up.'

'Yeah, Keira in that backless top is seared into my memory forever. Lesbian awakening,' she bantered back, refusing to be thrown off by Ellie's read.

'Guys, let's go,' Vee, swinging her car keys with impatience, uninterested in speaking to Flynn.

Back at Vee's house they all sat with her mum in the stagnant air of the living room. Rhiannon was less scared of her now, just felt deeply sorry for her, and when Vee explained that Isla liked to listen to their chatter she tried to give off an effervescence she didn't feel. Ellie began to tell Isla about her horses, and Isla asked Rhiannon if she too had animals.

'Yeah, I've got a Shetland pony and a Kelpie.'

'A kelpie? Nae, the poor thing. How wis hid brought out here? Passes as naught but a horse does hid?'

Rhiannon was confused and Vee stepped in. 'Nae, Mither, not that kind of kelpie.'

'What's she referring to?' Ellie asked, and after Vee explained about Scottish kelpies Ellie said, 'They sound like bunyips here. Like another water-based myth created to keep kids away from places that they might drown in.'

'Depends on who you ask I suppose, as to whether or not it's a myth,' Rhiannon said.

'Why, are bunyips from Dreaming stories?'

'Yeah. And I guess if selkies and kelpies are real, who's to say bunyips aren't? I suppose the original people of any place have more knowledge than anyone later ever gives them credit for.'

'True that,' Ellie said.

'How much time have we got till your mum comes to grab you guys? Did you want to watch a movie in my room?' Vee asked Ellie.

'Yeah, we've got like two hours. I think she's coming around five.'

'Are you gonna go to that doof tonight still?'

'Yeah! Please come. It's not like a proper doof, just a small thing out at Boggy Creek. Essie and Nat are coming too.'

'Na, I'm gonna stay in with my mum,' and as Vee said this she reached for her mother's hand, and Isla's fingers curled around her daughter's.

Isla's mind slipped back to eighteen years before, when she had slipped out of her sealskin so as to feel the novelty of sand between her toes, unsteady on her new legs she invoked the vulnerability and charm of a fawn, tripping up the beach, her body long limbed and split with crevices, like the gaps in the walls of rock rising around her in which the kittiwakes nested. As they screamed and circled, feeding sand eels to their chicks, a man surfaced out of the water nearby, with a strange board in hand, the same board that she had sometimes seen from underneath the waves, and wondered what bizarre rites humans practised upon them, or was it some kind of play? He looked at her and she looked at him and she felt her need drip down her thighs, knew she wanted the novelty of feeling something fill up that slit between her legs, knew she would be steadier on all fours, as she would be now for him. Unheeding of the warnings, because she was young and wanted him, she took him beneath the cliffs, the soft corpses of infant birds that had toppled off their ledge and the smashed shells of the eggs they had been expelled from crunching beneath her feet, a sensation as new as his pink dick inside her, and the mingling sweat of skin on skin.

For weeks they had met daily, and she grew to trust him, speaking of her life beneath the waves and no longer hiding her sealskin in mounds of seaweed but laying it down as a robe to fuck on and then to warm them as they lay. She had grown to love him too, spoke of them settling down in Orkney so they could continue their love affair forever, to dream of braving the unknown waters of the Southern Hemisphere, to see another land with him. Though as the time passed and her waist thickened she grew restless; moulting season had passed and she was impatient to roam, knowing she would be back later in the year for breeding season.

But he couldn't bear the thought of a babe born exposed on the rocks, knowing from what she told him that it wouldn't be a selkie like her, but a half creature, more human than not, abandoned on the beach, bare and discarded like the dead gulls they copulated beside. He couldn't bear the thought of losing her either, could see the sea held her more than he did, and so he had snatched her sealskin and taken her back with him to Australia, his pregnant bride.

Isla held on tightly to the one good thing she had got from it all, her daughter.

Ellie, Rhiannon and Vee were hours deep into *True Blood* when they heard the sound of tyres on gravel. Slightly annoyed by the interruption, but also eager for the night ahead, Rhiannon and Ellie gave hasty goodbyes and ran out to Sasha. As she reversed out of the driveway a car was waiting to pull in, and she stopped to let it move first. It was Vee's dad, Paul, and he stared at Sasha, frozen as if in shock, behind the curve of his wheel.

'Fucking idiot,' Sasha muttered under her breath when she saw he wasn't going to move, and speedily reversed back into the culvert and drove off. Looking back, Ellie and Rhiannon could see he was following the car with his locked gaze. Something about his expression gave an immediate and strange significance to the two girls.

'Who was that?!' Ellie demanded of her mum.

Rhiannon pretended to think the question was for her, smoothly said 'Vee's dad.'

'No, who was that to you, Sasha? Why was he looking so much?'

Sasha was silent for a moment, and then answered rushed and tersely, perhaps with a sudden compulsion to be free of the habit of secrecy.

'That was a client of mine. I think that was obvious to all of us, right Rhi?' She added, reminding her daughter of the presence of a guest. But Ellie didn't care, she broke into angry sobs and began to upbraid her mother, scolding her for the shame she had brought on her. Rhiannon stayed awkwardly silent for the forty-minute drive home, and all Sasha responded with was a caustic 'get it all out.'

As they let Rhiannon out at her house, she turned to Ellie and asked abashed, 'Did you still want to go out tonight?'

'Of course!' Ellie said, through a face damp from tears. 'Nat's brother is picking us up at ten,' and she pulled the door closed on Rhiannon's uncertain face.

14

When Ellie first got home she dashed upstairs, threw herself on her bed and cried loudly, hoping her mother would hear and know how much she had harmed her. After some time passed her sobbing eased though, as much as she tried to prolong it, and she was almost disgruntled that Sasha hadn't come to check on her. She thought of skipping dinner as a statement, but she was hungry and where else would she eat? There was no way she would go seek comfort at Rhiannon's in the way Rhiannon sought comfort at hers.

She came downstairs in stony silence, ready to flounce off at any moment. Sasha and her so rarely fought that the whole situation seemed absurd – she felt as if she were acting a mother/daughter part that could crack at any moment, and she saw in the wry raise of an eyebrow that her mother was over her antics but would humour them. She was embarrassed by the way she had behaved in the car, wishing she had taken the higher ground and lectured her wayward mother rather than falling to pieces. She had undermined her own arguments. Not that she had any collected arguments – she just knew that what Sasha was doing was deeply wrong, because she *felt* it was wrong, she didn't need to justify why.

After a few minutes with only the sound of their chewing, Sasha said, 'Did you want to talk about it?'

Ellie slammed her cutlery down and launched into speech; 'how could you do this to me? Do you have any idea of the way people are going to speak to me, treat me? I'm already the odd one out, being Eurasian, and now you've got to condemn me with this too. It's not like you don't have other options! You could actually *be* a receptionist like you told me you were. I've got to carry shame from you now too.'

'Ellie, it's understandable to be upset and frustrated. Firstly, because I kept it from you. I should never have lied, at least not for this long. You were old enough to understand a long time ago, but I was afraid to tell you. That's something I regret. And secondly, because you're right, society sees sex work as a mark of shame upon a whole family, and people do sometimes punish children for who their parents are. But don't you think it's unfair though Ellie, the way that society holds mothers to impossible standards? That we are supposed to be somehow virginal, inviolate, perfect women. I think your anger at me is partially misplaced frustration for that. It does pain me that people's prejudices extend to you –'

'Ellie opened her mouth to interrupt. 'But,' said Sasha, holding up her hand, unwilling to pause the torrent of words that she'd been practising in her head for years, trying to defend herself to society via her daughter, Ellie a stand in for a wider imagined audience. 'Let me finish. This is not something I have done to you. I haven't done something malicious, or intentional or even directed at you. I've made life decisions that are adjacent to you, and affect your life in good and bad ways. The bad, you've just expressed. The good, you can see all around you – in this home we have and the lifestyle you live. And consider this; I haven't always had the options I have now; I was a teen mum. If I had done a normal job, as a single mum, I wouldn't have had the financial stability I've had or, more importantly, the time to be around you that I've had. And those things matter more to me than other people's opinions of how I should live my life.'

'Okay, fine. Not how can you do this to me then, but how can you do this to *yourself*? It's disgusting and immoral, how can you sleep with so many men? Aren't you grossed out?'

'There are many jobs that can be disgusting, Ellie. Cleaning toilets, being a nurse that has to treat bedsores. That doesn't make them immoral. I'm not ruining the planet, like mining magnates are, or committing atrocities against people in other nations, like the military is –'

'Yes you are! You're ruining marriages.'

'Those marriages were already ruined, long before my clients come to me. I am not actively seeking out married men. They are actively seeking me out.'

'Yeah and they're *revolting*! How can you get with them?'

'Ellie, there are worse things in life than sleeping with unattractive men. Most of the women in the world are sleeping with unattractive men – men are by default, and as a whole, generally unattractive. Do you ask every woman you pass on the street, walking alongside a gross man who is obviously her husband, 'Yuck, how can you bring yourself to sleep with such a repulsive man?''

'No, but they can at least respect themselves. They can have dignity. There's no dignity in what you do.'

'Dignity? Oh Ellie. Dignity is overrated. Dignity is all about other people finding you respectable, seeing things in you that *they* deem are worthy of respect. I've got integrity, I'm guided by my own morals and I stay true to them. I respect myself, and I hope one day you'll be able to respect me too, but if you don't, that's not my problem. And why do you find marriage, which has historically been about economic security, all that respectable anyway? Because women marry *one* man for financial security, instead of sleeping with many? Because we've been told that's the respectable and right way to do things? Why?'

'Okay, okay, you don't need to speak to me like we're at a debating competition or something, geez.'

'You saying that coz you feel like you lost the imagined debate?' Sasha teased.

'Whatever. Let's not talk about it anymore. How cold is it gonna be tonight? Do you think I need to wear stockings?'

Sasha smiled as she answered, and reached for her pouch to roll a durry.

That night Rhiannon didn't bring up what had happened, figured Ellie wanted to put it behind her and just immerse herself in the party. It was a small setup, just an illegal gathering in the state forest, only had to pay $5 on entry to help cover the cost of the speakers the organisers had rented and lugged out in the back of a ute. Fifteen or so cars hemmed them in, cordoning off the unofficial dancefloor. As the night went on it got cooler, and they compensated with alcohol, sitting in Nat's brother's car sculling straight from the sack, watching people crawl out of boots on arrival because their cars were short of seats. Esther arrived at midnight completely wasted with a bunch of Coffs guys they didn't know and a gram of MDMA, which she generously shared. They put the back seats down and rolled around in the back of the car, munted and gossiping.

'There's two guys sitting on the bonnet of the car,' Ellie said.

'My brother will hate that, let's get them off,' Nat clambered through to the front seat and began to honk the horn, but neither budged.

'Fuck it, just leave them. That horn is so annoying,' Rhiannon said. 'It's so nice and warm in here I honestly just wanna stay here all night, would that be sad?'

'We could just stay in here till like 4am and go out for the morning set,' Nat suggested.

'Shhh, guys, let's try hear what these cunts are saying,' Esther wound down the window and a sliver of cold air came in with the voices.

'... the way you get a hot girl is go for a heaps insecure one and then she'll be grateful as that she got you. The more insecure the better. Endless gobbies, man, and finger barrels galore,' one boy said to the other, and they both laughed.

'Oh my god, Rhi, it's that guy who stuck his fingers up my pussy at that house party!' Ellie whispered, elbowing her.

'Yuck, wind the window back up, they're disgusting.'

They kept drinking, got increasingly euphoric and felt like they were at the centre of the party, the most sought-after spot. No one could be having as much fun as them! Till Esther broke the mirage with a restless, 'I'm pretty keen for a dance hey, any of youse wanna come?'

'Naaaa,' Nat answered, after looking at the other two questioningly, and seeing they were cuddled together under a rug they had found in the boot.

'Okay well I'm gonna go.'

'You sure you'll be sweet by yourself?'

'Yeah, I'll just find the boys I came with, they're always in amongst it. Catch ya,' she slammed the door behind her.

Hours later they turned on the ignition to check the time on the car radio and saw it was 4.12am and began to shake up their stiff legs and munch the muesli bars they found in the glovebox in preparation for leaving. Ellie refused to give up the rug and added it to her look, stepping out with the moth-eaten rag around her shoulders like a cloak.

'Very doof chic,' Nat complimented.

The dancefloor had about two dozen people on it, and Esther was right at the front, twisting her hands in slowly oscillating patterns in front of her face. As her hands crossed into the light from the stage Ellie noticed they had something on them, caked up to the elbows, but she couldn't tell what in the darkness.

'Essie, what's on your hands?'

But Esther was too fucked up to even speak, only gave a dopey smile in response and hugged Ellie.

As they danced the clearing gradually lightened, passing to a soft, murky grey that heralded the beginning of the day. They couldn't hear the carolling of the magpies with the psytrance so loud, but the laughter of the kookaburras penetrated through. Esther's coated arms slowly became tinged with colour as the sun rose, till they were clearly a rusty brown.

Ellie held Esther's hands, gazed at them worriedly, and then displayed them to the others. 'Guys, it's dried blood. She's covered in blood. Essie are you okay?'

'Has she cut herself?' Nat began to look over her arms, turning them this way and that as Esther kept shuffling from foot to foot, in a rhythmic sway as close to a dance as she could get in that state.

'She seems happy enough... she's obviously not in pain... and I can't see anything,' Rhiannon said.

'I don't know, this is really suss. I think when the sun is up properly we should have more of a look,' Ellie took the rug off her shoulders and wrapped it around Esther, who didn't even have a jumper on.

Half an hour later it was light enough to really see, and Ellie pointed out that there were streaks down her legs too, and stains around the bottom of her dress, a silk shift designed for the boudoir not the dancefloor. By this point Ellie was deeply concerned over the mystery, and taking things into her own hands she marched up to one of the guys who had brought Esther and asked if he knew why she had blood all over her.

'Not sure hey but she was passed out in the tray of my ute for a bit there, maybe check that. It's parked over there,' he pointed to it, a white one behind a bunch of other cars to the left of the stage.

Rhiannon and Ellie left Nat to look after Esther and set off, interested to see the contours of the terrain that they had stumbled through in the night. It was mainly bracken fern, crushed beneath many feet, and blackberry brambles that explained the slight scratches on both their ankles. Coming up to the muddy ute they peeked over the edge into the tray. It was smeared in blood, and in one corner there was a small pool of it filled with floating chunks of some kind. They were both shocked into silence for half a track, music clamouring insistently in their ears, adding a grim reality of the now to what they saw.

'Jeeesus *Christ* that's a lot of blood...' Rhiannon walked around the other side to look more closely at it. 'Do you think she could've been pregnant?' She put words to what they were both, inevitably, thinking.

As they continued to stare they instinctively reached for each other's hand, grasping at comfort in the face of something that had so irrevocably shifted the mood of the party. A gothic gruesomeness had entered their little world and put an edge to the high they were still feeling.

'Pretty bleak. Should we tell her?' Ellie finally brought herself to speak.

'Na, at least not anytime soon. Let's just clean the blood off her now so she doesn't get freaked out when she sobers up a bit. If she asks anything about it later we can tell her.'

Ellie took Rhiannon's arm gently in hers, and they walked back to the dancefloor, more mournful than how they'd left it, but ready to dance, scrub the blood off their friend with the help of a water bottle, and warm themselves in the bright sun of a new day.

15

Second term was starting back in two days, and Rhiannon was making the most of the solitary time. She lay on the trampoline looking up at the crisp blue of an autumn sky, marred only by clouds around McGrath's Hump, in an odd torn up conglomeration that reminded her of the Dead Marshes that Gollum was currently guiding Frodo and Sam through in her reread. She had paused mid page to roll onto her back, gaze into the heavens and let her mind wander. Above her swallows flitted, and she could see a hawk hovering over the horse paddock and hear the piercing cry of a whip bird from the rainforest. It would be cold in the shade of all those tall trees now, only the mulch from the rotting leaves and logs would be letting out any heat, housing centipedes and fungi in the warmth of the rainforest floor. She thought of the trail rides Ellie and her had taken up the fire trails, the damp earth the horses' hooves overturned with a neat flick, the way they had to dismount on the steep parts and let them slide their way down the slippery leaves and mud. The way the forest seemed to close around them, claustrophobic vines that grabbed at them as they went past and the unrelenting vibration of the cicadas.

Ajax dozed in the full sun of the verandah and she thought of how Vee had accepted her Facebook relationship status request last night. They were now Facebook official, there for anyone and everyone to see – there had been a mass move from Myspace to the new platform at the beginning of the year so it was, really, everyone. She had even managed to talk Vee into creating a profile. She did miss the personalised aspect of Myspace though, missed the way Death Cab for Cutie would play every time she looked at her page. Had no idea that it would remain there, frozen in time, for a decade; that there would be a trail of her across the internet, from her days of RPG forums through to the rise of social media corporations. This change marked the end of the wild west of the internet, the frontier days that she had grown up with, and soon it would be choked with advertising and algorithms and censorship. Angela was gone for the morning, had attempted to bribe Rhiannon to go with her, 'I'll buy you a magazine if you come do the grocery shopping with me.' Rhiannon had declined, knowing it was never what it seemed, and also resenting her for not just being forthright. Why not say 'would you come into town with me, I want help with the shopping?' She would've respected that request and gone. Her mum only knew how to barter, and devalued any answer in the process. It was never 'could you please do the washing up' but 'if you don't do the washing up I'll cut your pocket money' or 'if you do the washing up I'll rent you a DVD tomorrow,' assuming the worst of Rhiannon as if she couldn't communicate through any other means. She saw the way Sasha communicated with Ellie, and the way she communicated with her own friends, and knew there was another way. She'd never heard her mum apologise in her life, only make excuses and dodge responsibility, always blaming her father. The only 'sorry' to come from her mouth was weaponised and false – 'I am so sorry I've given birth to an autistic daughter' or 'I'm sorry for you that you take so much after your father.' In reaction to this Rhiannon was acutely aware of accountability, overly ready to apologise and flatten herself for someone else, hated receiving favours in case they had a catch, felt distrustful of random acts of kindness and was so transparent about desires that it became a bluntness bordering on rudeness. Only her friendships softened her, otherwise she bristled with a fierce independence, an independence that she had seen in Vee too, and maybe it was that more than anything else that had drawn the standoffish girl to her. They had seen a strength in each other that made them cleave to one another; or maybe it wasn't that meaningful, maybe they had just been stirred by teen hormones, their respective pheromones pulling them in more than personality.

Anyway, it didn't matter how it had happened, it had happened. And now she laid back and luxuriated in the memory of Vee, felt her with her everywhere she went, as if she were a bouquet stirred into life by her presence, even felt her in her fingers now, as they rested on the edge of her underwear, contemplating the things they could do but were better off saved for her, confident that she would see her in a few days, confident in the way that she would touch her.

She must've fallen asleep because she awoke to find her mum standing on the verandah, looking at the half-healed scars that Rhiannon hadn't been able to hide. She was groggy from her nap but her throat immediately constricted and her stomach tightened, just as her mind clouded into a haze of panic. There were a few beats of silence in which she could hear the call of a bell bird, the rush of the river and even felt she could hear the tug of the cows' tongues ripping out blades of grass, and then her mum went in.

'I can see now why you're such a slut, you can't help it, you've been damaged. I knew there was something wrong with you. But you can't hide it from me. I know that you've been...' There was a litany of supposed things she'd done and she tried to block it out while knowing that her silence would escalate it, feeling like she was in a catch-22, wanted to seek refuge in the mouse holes in the hedge that she could just see out of the corner of her eye, imagined herself as the mouse looking out from within, seeing the legs of the trampoline with beads of condensation from where the grass met the metal, unable to see the two women but only to hear their breath and voices. One accusation shattered her fantasy though, threw her out from that distanced perspective and back into her own, blasted it across her brain and came to prominence, in stark neon letters that pulsed with an unnatural glare. 'I know you've been sleeping with your father.' She couldn't escape *that* and instantaneously she knew that she had to leave, somehow, leave this most beautiful place in the world, this property that she loved, because the situation was untenable, it had gone too far, how could she even defend herself, how could that even be thought of her? What misdirected pain or guilt *was* that?

She had no memory of how the tirade ended, how much longer it went for, she could only remember getting out. She thought of killing herself, like she did so much, and then cut herself instead, it was her saviour, which other people never understood. She set off walking to

Ellie's, numb the whole way, just as her bare feet were numb on the roads in the autumn air.

Later that day, feeling shell-shocked and curled up in bed with Ellie, Rhiannon began to shake. Unable to cry, her body shook with what was unshed, and she felt as though she was watching from outside of it, had stepped out and that's why she couldn't move, couldn't answer when Ellie asked if she was okay. She pressed the recent cuts on her arm till the pain of it brought her back into herself. Ellie must've said something to her mum, because over dinner Sasha said to her, 'You can stay as long as you like, Rhi.'

She went home the next afternoon to grab her school books and be ready for the first day of term. She wasn't ready to leave her home. Yet. As she packed her school bag she listened to Dolly Parton on her iPod, and thought of the way her nostalgia for her mountain home wound like a country road through all the songs that Rhiannon loved most, and how that same nostalgia must stagnate in Isla's heart, turning the waters polluted and brackish. It gave her a whole new perspective on Isla. How trapped she must feel, and how exiled from the place she loved. No wonder she drank so much; the alcohol not only dulled but also reflected the displacement she felt within. She was sick with it and from it all, and something had to be done. At school the next day she raised it tentatively with Ellie.

'Ellie, you know how Vee's dad is a client of your mum? And he obviously knows where the sealskin is? What if we got her to help us in some way? Like to find it for Isla.'

Ellie was at first resistant. She understood now that her mother's job wasn't innately a bad thing, but she couldn't see anything positive in it. She still felt disapproval, even though she knew her disapproval was unwarranted. But then she allowed that maybe it was a possibility, or at least worth bringing up with Sasha. She promised she would. They said nothing to Vee, not wanting to get her hopes up. That night though, Ellie called Rhiannon excitedly, babbling about her mother being in. Ellie hadn't told her mum the whole story, Sasha could just readily accept that here was a relationship that a woman needed help escaping from, that it didn't need to be visible or violent to be abusive, and also saw an opportunity to reunite with her daughter.

On Wednesday at school, secreted away in Vee's car on a free period they all shared, Rhiannon and Ellie told their idea to her. Not remotely surprised to hear her dad was a client of Sasha's, she was grateful, but not entirely hopeful.

'How is she able to help?'

'She just said she'll be able to get any info we need from him; she has a hold over him or something.'

'What if he's destroyed it? Like burned it or something?'

'Well, I guess then we know for sure, which is still better than not knowing right?'

'I suppose...'

That evening, when Rhiannon got home from school, the shadows already lay long across the paddocks. She rushed to light the fire, scrabbling with the kindling in her arms. She was determined to get a call in with Vee before dinner, and didn't want to use the home phone where she would be overheard. She marched a kilometre up the hill to where she could get reception on her mobile and the neighbour's Brangus cows looked at her with kind curiosity, their long ears and dewlaps hanging when she climbed on to the fence post near them. She preferred the purebred Angus but the Brahmin crosses meant tick resistance, and supposedly handled the buffalo flies better – those horrible midges that drove the cows to tear their necks open in desperation on fence posts, rubbing at an itch they could never quell. There was usually a blue-tongued lizard sunning himself there too, that scurried away when she came near, but he must've disappeared into hibernation.

Vee called her when she texted, and Rhiannon furled herself around her phone, knees up around her ears and hugging her girlfriend's comforting tones to her. They spoke of the great beyond, what would happen if Isla was freed and Rhi escaped her mum, what they could do, the life they could create, a queer dreaming that unfolded between them and that they treasured as carefully as each other. Rhiannon could see that she had a future ahead of her other than hating herself and her life, that maybe she came from a failed family unit but that wasn't the end of it, and she bridled as she spoke, imagining asserting herself in front of her mum for the first and final time, declaring that she was moving out. She began to feel that maybe her emancipation was caught up with Isla's, and the two twined in her mind till it was Vee, whom she loved and adored, that was saving them both. Rhiannon looked at the tattered ear of the cow closest to her, where its ear tag had torn out, and tried to read the branded number within it as her hands froze on the phone and she knew she had to walk back for dinner.

16

The first two weeks back at school were difficult for both Ellie and Esther. News had spread about Sasha's job and Esther's miscarriage through the school holidays, and now they were both taunted by their peers. Ellie suffered under ruthless teasing, whereas Esther's persecution was less transparent, more maliciousness disguised as condescending care, though she really didn't seem to care and bit back with an eagerness that showed no signs of being rattled. When Cam played up his sorrow, said he was sorry for her loss in a hushed voice and how traumatic it must've been, she waved his concerns away with a flick of her wrist, dismissed them with an, 'Oh please, I was so high I couldn't even feel it. I was almost as high as you were in that photo I saw on Facebook the other day – who took that by the way?'

Esther had only spoken with Rhiannon, Ellie and Keira without the protection of sarcasm. She told them she was relieved more than anything – it would've been a nuisance to deal with otherwise – and reassured Keira that it hadn't been from her threesome with her and Flynn.

'People keep saying it must've been awful but what's so awful about it, really? Just a lot of blood. I didn't want to be pregnant and I didn't even know I was, so it's not like I lost anything. And surely a medically induced abortion is just as bad if not worse on your body and mind?'

'I totally get what you're saying, I think people are just confronted by women being messy. And there's something about the publicness of it... but really it's no different morally,' Rhiannon said. 'It makes me think of traditional medicine practices, like the plants that women have taken for thousands of years to bring on a miscarriage, that aren't accepted by the Western World. Like obviously wouldn't recommend that widely coz you need to have the knowledge for the correct dosing, and it could be dangerous otherwise. But yeah. There are ways to have our bodies do things outside of a doctor's office.'

They were sitting in the smoking area, a small courtyard coming off the quad, on the third Tuesday of term, and as Rhiannon finished speaking, Vee and Zoe walked up, lit durries in hand.

'Can I scab a ciggie?' asked Esther, shameless. She was known to hover around the smoking area waiting for smokers.

Zoe passed her one and flashed her a smile. Her cheek piercings sparkled in place of dimples.

'I've always loved those dermal piercings of yours,' Esther said.

'Oh my god, that reminds me. Guess what I got over the weekend? Nipple piercings! I went to Pushkar, here let me show you,' and Zoe began to pull down her low-cut top and heave each breast out of her bra, where the bell bars twinkled like the nose ring of a pig's soft pink snout offsetting and contrasting with the harsh metal.

'Hot,' they all agreed and 'did it hurt?!' and 'I can't believe I'm finally getting to see your rack!' from Ellie and Vee.

'A bit, but not heaps. Not as much as my clit did...'

'Wait, you got your clit done too?! Don't you have to be eighteen for that??'

'Yeah, fully, but the guy didn't ask for ID. And I just got the hood. Can't touch it for ages though, don't know how I'm going to masturbate. I've got, like, blue balls.'

'I get you. I can't sleep without it,' Esther said.

'Could you try just running a cold water tap directly on it, with your legs spread under the faucet? If the water pressure is strong enough I can come that way,' Ellie said.

'Oh yeah, maybe I'll try that!'

'Except,' she added, in a serious tone, 'look out coz once I accidentally bumped the hot water tap as I was coming and burned my clit! It was fucked.'

'Oh my god that reminds me of when I got this skin infection from this guy I fucked, called Molluscum Contagium, it looks kind of like school sores, and they were all over my pussy and I had one on my clit and the way they treat it is by burning it off with that stuff they use to burn warts off, liquid nitrogen,' they all stared in horror as Esther spoke, able to tell where the story was headed, 'and he had to burn my clit with the nitrogen! It was so fucked. And way more traumatic than that miscarriage people won't stop fucking talking about.' In typical Esther fashion she had them all laughing at her flippancy.

A guy from their year walked past and, as their laughter eased, quipped, 'Hey Ellie, heard your mum's a MILF, any chance you can book me in with her? I can give you your cut now as down payment. And how about mates' rates hey, coz I'm at your school and all?'

Ellie shrank into the shadows of the girls around her and didn't respond, but Esther and Zoe turned on him with a viciousness he deserved, and told him to go fuck himself, saying they would set their older brothers on him if he didn't leave them the hell alone.

As he disappeared around the corner Zoe turned to Esther. 'You have an older brother too? I didn't realise. What school did he go to?'

'I don't have one. But he doesn't know that. Just works to shut them up.' They all laughed again, Ellie joining in despite her mortification. The joke was on him now.

On Saturday, Ellie, Rhiannon, Vee and Nat wandered through the Bello Markets. It thronged with people, and though most of the stalls didn't interest them anymore and they just browsed and critiqued, it was always a chance to run into someone they hadn't seen in ages. It was quite cold under the camphor laurels though and after forty minutes and a lap of the oval they grew bored.

'What should we do? There's nothing on tonight.'

'I wouldn't be able to go out tonight anyway. I've still got that

English assignment to do. Want to go back to mine and hang?' Nat offered. The others agreed and they set off up Church Street, relishing the spokes of sun gushing through breaks in the trees overhead, and down towards Lavenders Bridge. Halfway across though Nat paused. 'I just realised my mum is home, I better check with her that she wants a whole group of people before we rock up. Sometimes she doesn't like it.'

They waited while she called her mum, all three of them leaning over the railings with the bar pressing their stomachs in. The memory of jumping into the water felt far away. Was that really something they did over the summer? The autumn temperature distanced them.

'It's a no go, I'm sorry guys. Wanna just go hang at The Point instead? It shouldn't be crowded this time of year.'

The Point was a bend in the river a ten-minute walk upstream from the bridge, with a rope swing and a deep swimming hole. A favourite place to pull bongs, it was often littered with empty beer bottles and other careless trash. They walked towards it, going past the caravan park and the pungent stench of Bat Island, where most of the town's flying foxes roosted by day. Nat fell back to walk with Rhiannon, who was straggling.

'You know my mum is close friends with your mum?'

'No, I didn't know,' Rhiannon said.

'Yeah they do book club together... she said I wasn't allowed to bring you round. That you're "trouble" or something stupid.'

There was an awkward pause while Rhiannon overcame her shock and hurt. 'What did she say exactly?'

'Something about you being a slut and sleeping around with guys, she didn't want me being influenced.'

'But I'm a lesbian?'

'Yeah, I mean I know that, it's obviously stupid. Anyway, I just thought you should know.'

Once they got to The Point they threw rocks aimlessly into the centre of the current, and only Vee actually braved the waters, taking her clothes off and swimming in her underwear to the far side.

'This could fully be *Deliverance* country, couldn't it?' Rhiannon said to Ellie.

'Totally. I think it's the pines hanging over the water. And the river is murkier than it is out in Thora... Sasha said she can give us a lift home in like an hour if we want to go then by the way. I'm going to go coz I need to write my history assignment.'

'Yeah, let's do that. I know Vee has to do her English one too, so I don't want to ask her to drive us that far.'

Vee began to swim back over, clumsily stepped out and drip dried on the stones, each splash changing them from bone white to dark grey. 'So, what's the plan?'

'We're gonna head home after this. What are you up to tomorrow though?'

'Well, if I get this assignment finished I'll be free.'

'How don't you have any to do, Rhi?' Nat asked.

'She's always finished before anyone else has even started, such a nerd,' Ellie answered for her.

'Too smart for her own good,' Vee said, and pulled Rhiannon towards her for a reluctant kiss.

'Why don't we go to Dorrigo for a walk tomorrow if it's a clear day?' Ellie suggested, looking up at the plateau they could just see peeking out at the top of the mountain range.

'Yeah, I'm down to drive us,' Vee said.

'I won't be able to come, I've got a society and culture assignment to write too,' Nat was forlorn, 'So boring. But youse go.'

Early the next morning Vee picked up Rhiannon and Ellie. They were all rugged up in winter jackets, even though it was only May. It was often ten degrees colder up on the mountain, and sometimes even snowed as close as Ebor. As the car climbed, twisting through the narrow turns of Waterfall Way, their ears blocked and popped through the change in altitudes. The view unfolded below them in sections of road unobstructed by thick rainforest trees. They could see all of Bellingen, an island of light green among the dark, stretching to the horizon. At numerous points they had to wait while oncoming traffic went first; the road became one way as waterfalls falling from the tops dashed over the edge, continuing their drop to the valley far below. Rhiannon and Ellie had swum at the bottom of one such fall; they weren't sure which though, they had done a treacherous rock climb up the Never Never River, to see Gleniffer Falls at its source. It had taken them six hours and Ellie had cried part way, said she didn't have the strength to make it, after doggy paddling through a seemingly bottomless pool with possessions on her head and crawling up a steep rock ledge, slippery with moss and insects scuttling.

When they reached the top of the mountain there were rolling hills and hedges, maintained as windbreaks, dividing the paddocks into neat shapes. A thick fog partially obscured it all, so that it felt like only sky and hill, enormous and unending.

'Wow, you can see why this area is called New England,' Vee said. They pulled over on a wide gravel verge to take it all in.

'Have you ever brought your mum up here? I know it's not the same as Orkney but maybe similar vibes,' Rhiannon said.

'Na, I haven't. It might just make her homesickness worse.'

Rhiannon pulled back onto the road and they passed by fields of cows and potatoes, true cultivated farming country barely discernible in the mist, but all surrounded by ancient Gondwana rainforests, older than the continent itself. They turned towards the rainforest centre and then took a left to get to the Rosewood Creek walk, which always had less people than the Crystal Showers Falls walk. As they stomped beneath the towering trees, some of them thousands of years old and survivors of the age of logging that desecrated the Northern Tablelands they chattered, not quite as loudly as the chorus of birds around them but enough to warn any oncoming animals to stay hidden. Only brave brush turkeys crossed their path, and leeches grasped at their jeans as they went by.

'There must be so many weed crops hidden out here. Sasha's guy has his in the state forest and coz there are Indigenous rangers that go through to find any trees of cultural significance before logging starts he says they always end up finding it, and taking some – which is fair really. He always jokes that he only gets a third of the crop he plants – coz the rangers take a third and then the wallabies eat a third.' Ellie suddenly changed topics. 'After this we should go see Ebor Falls, It's less than an hour's drive. I haven't been there in so long. Are you up for that, Vee?'

'Oh yeah, I'm so fine to drive more, I'm not tired at all.'

Prehistoric ferns dampened their denim with a kiss as they brushed by, and each creek that sparkled over the path, forcing them to rock hop, seemed like a fairy's bath, a glen fit for any nymph queen to wash her ankles in, to tie her hair up to dry in the spattering of sunlight flickering through. Rhiannon wondered what could be seen if she stayed behind and kept still, so still that she became part of the landscape. How many days would she have to stay till the forest grew used to her, let itself grow around her? Would Vee have better luck than her? Would the sprites sense a kindred being, someone else forged from magic and nature beyond human comprehension? Would they come out and play in front of her, would they be thoughtless and frolicsome?

She remained contemplative on the drive to Ebor, watched the country turn brown and dry as they passed beyond the highest point, where the clouds of orographic rain always punctured and spilled upon the earth towards the coast. Ebor Falls was impressive, mighty gallons of water thundering over the cliff face, that sprayed upon their own faces. And afterwards they strolled through the cemetery adjacent to it, with wooden crosses slowly rotting into the earth and Victorian gravestones softened with lichens.

'I'd like to be buried here when I die, so I can hear the sound of the falls. What a beautiful graveyard,' she said.

'I think you have to be a local resident... I think there's quite strict zoning laws with burying these days.' Ellie said apologetically.

'Okay, well then scatter my ashes over Ebor Falls.'

On the way back down the mountain they were accompanied by the smell of burning rubber, from the trucks ahead that had their brakes on the whole way down. It would be a terrifying slope to lose control on, so steep and winding, and Rhiannon remembered a story of the remains of a cart that was found at the base of the mountain, when the road had to be reconstructed after a rock fall, with the skeleton of a horse still harnessed in, and the skeleton of a woman too. They must've toppled over the edge who knows how long ago, and Rhiannon thought of the man who rode his brumby up and down the mountain because he'd been banned from Dorrigo pub, how he tied the horse out the back of Bellingen pub and went home drunk at night, because the brumby could find its way through the rainforest and he couldn't get a DUI mounted on it. She thought of Isla's alcoholism too, and turned to Ellie.

'How do you think your mum is gonna get the info we need from Vee's dad?'

'I don't know yet, she told me she's working on an idea.'

'Guess we'll just have to be patient,' said Vee, though the tap of her fingers on the steering wheel belied that.

17

Weeks passed, and time was only marked by the assignments they handed in and the gaining of P plates. Those with birthdays later in the year were intensely jealous of anyone who turned seventeen in the first half and were able to drive without a parent, the first step towards independence in a country area. As May became June, Ellie and Rhiannon both noted the early Thora frosts. They left Ellie undoing horse rugs with ice cold buckles that seared her hands, and Rhiannon defrosting Angela's windscreen with a bucket of hot water thrown over it. Grass cracked under their feet in the mornings and Rhiannon's favourite frangipani died when she forgot to cover it in hessian and its sap froze. At school they bought hot pizza rounders from the canteen for lunch and held them in elated hands.

With the season came an excuse to keep her scarred arms covered and Rhiannon had developed a routine with her mum: get home, endure an accusation, cut, go to bed, go to school, never cry. She found she craved it. Cutting gave her a high. The only thing that made her hesitate was Vee's hurt whenever she noticed a new one, the one person who saw her completely undressed in the winter.

They had no news from Sasha yet, and the three of them had stopped speaking about it. On days her mum wasn't around Rhiannon lit the fire in the afternoon, sat in the living room and gazed into it for hours, hypnotised by the crackle of flames. 'I want Mordor,' she said to Ellie once with glee, and they built it as high as it would go, till it burnt the back of their legs as they stood before it.

Ellie complained to her about having to heat a kettle in the feed room first to mix the horses' morning feed with boiling water, otherwise her hands got too cold from the tap. She had Gemma stabled at night, because she was getting old and struggled to keep weight on, and so came onto the bus every day not just smelling of hay and pulling wisps of it out of her pockets, but straw too, golden dust sprinkled in her dark hair.

Through all this Vee kept swimming, showing up every day with wet hair, evoking the mysterious girl that Rhiannon had first fallen for. They had been together for six months now, but their honeymoon period carried on. They still couldn't get enough of each other's bodies, perhaps because they never were able to overindulge, living too far apart to spend every evening together, or even most evenings. It still took wrangling, and Rhiannon spent long days alone out in Thora, days when she couldn't be bothered to walk the six kilometres to Ellie's or even meet her halfway, days in which she savoured being solitary with her surrounds, taking Ajax on walks up the fire trails into the rainforest, masturbating to Radeo on the Suicide Girls website or reading a whole book in one sitting, prone on the trampoline.

One such a morning, a Saturday, Rhiannon got a call from Ellie. 'Keira just told me she's got a soccer match in Bello at midday. Want to go watch? We can hang with her after, and Sasha said she can take us.'

So they found themselves sitting on cold metal seats on the oval, cheering their friend on, feeling slightly traitorous as they knew a number of the girls on the Bello side. Keira was a talented striker, scoring two goals for her team. She seemed in her element as she sucked the juice from a quartered orange at half-time. A number of the girls on her team were Aboriginal, Orara having a far bigger Indigenous population than Bellingen, and Ellie and Rhiannon felt their ignorance when one girl called Keira 'sis' and they asked eagerly, 'Oh my god, is that your sister?' only to be told it wasn't literal – just lingo they weren't up with and wasn't meant for them. Afterwards Keira hobbled up into town with them in her soccer boots, studs uneven on the ground, scoring the pavement. They got pies at the Swiss Patiss, gobbled them up in the sun and lounged with full stomachs, feeling completely at ease. Till Keira went off to use the public bathrooms and returned with a strange look on her face.

'There's some graffiti in there I think youse guys might want to see...'

'Oh, you mean our names? We wrote them in there ages ago. In like year nine,' Ellie countered excitedly.

'No, not that, someone has added something to them,' she said as she gravely led them towards the toilets.

In the second cubicle, on the back of the door, were their names that they'd scrawled two years before. But beneath them, in harsh capitals of whiteout, someone had written WHORES DAUGHTER and DADDYS FUCK(ER).

Rhiannon felt so sick she was afraid she would vomit. Trying to regain some composure, she noted, 'They forgot the apostrophes.'

It wasn't till Keira got picked up by Flynn that she said anything else. She immediately turned to Ellie. 'Are people really thinking that about me, do you think?'

'I don't know, look, I doubt it. People just like a scandal, they'll write anything. How the hell did that rumour even get out there, though?'

'The only one it could've come from is my mum... she's the only person who could've spread it. And I know she said something about me to her book club coz Nat's mum was suss on me.'

'God, would you really say that about your own daughter, though?'

'If you hated the dad as much as she hates mine I guess you could... and I guess she's never been able to trust him with other women when they were together but *me*... the worst part is I have no idea if she actually believes it or if she's just saying it as like calumny. And I don't know which is worse... that she's delusional or just doesn't care about me being collateral.'

'Also, if you *were* sleeping with your dad you would be the victim of abuse...'

'Yeah... I wish people would ask me instead of just believing it. But I would also hate that, I don't want to talk about it with anyone, I just want it all to go away...'

Her sickness continued in Sasha's car on the way back to Thora, and it wasn't till they got to Ellie's that she realised it was the queasiness of the beginning of her period. Ellie suggested they each pull a cone and watch a movie, and so they put on *The Matrix*. About fifteen minutes in, the nausea in Rhiannon's lower belly increased to twinges of discomfort, and she excused herself to go to the bathroom. Sasha found her there ten minutes later, lying on the bathroom floor like a foetus and clutching her belly.

'Have you overdone it? You girls should never smoke too much in one sitting. It's like a child eating too many lollies from a jar; you'll make yourselves sick,' she said, assuming Rhiannon was greening out.

Rhiannon had never properly had period cramps before, and had no idea of how bad the pain could be, so she just curled further in on herself in the hope that would lessen the agony in her uterus. Sasha crouched down beside her, and then must've put two and two together. 'I'll get you a heat pack,' she said gently, and left the room.

She soon returned and helped Rhiannon to the lounge room, where she held the heat pack to Rhiannon's belly. 'Mine got worse at this age too,' she said. Sasha gave her some Nurofen and looked after her while Ellie was, presumably, passed out in a semi-stoned nap upstairs. Rhiannon sweated profusely, unable to tell what was coming from period pain and what was coming from being high. Through the spasms though she wished she could somehow stay there forever, being tended to by a woman older than her, who touched her with soft hands and didn't seem set against her.

Two days later Rhiannon was sitting with Cam in the quad. The two of them had wagged the second half of their society and culture class, a bludge of a subject that seemed to be mainly constituted of definitions of buzz words. They waited for everyone else to get out of class. Rhiannon rarely spent time with Cam one on one, and in fact often felt a bit guilty that he grated on her. Felt that she should have more solidarity for an overtly gay boy who couldn't hide his femininity. It was just that his penchant for gossip, coupled with the fact that he self-identified as a 'gossip' disconcerted her, she didn't quite trust it, or him. So when he said, 'Nat mentioned you don't have a good relationship with your mum' she at first prickled, and felt herself close off and a boundary come up, as if a sheet of Perspex glass had slid between them.

'Yep.'

He seemed to sense her reluctance, and with a delicacy she didn't think he was capable of, immediately clarified, 'I'm not asking you to talk about it, don't worry. It's just I've got a really difficult relationship with my mum too... and I've never spoken to anyone else who has one.'

She let out an inadvertent and surprised 'Oh.' He continued, talking about how hard it was to tell people, that he felt people didn't believe you when you said you had a bad mother, even though they unhesitatingly believed it if you said you had a bad father. He talked about how they questioned you, demanded what *you* must've done wrong to create the situation. He spoke about his determination not to be like his mother, but his fears that he was inevitably becoming her anyway were inexorable. 'She lies so much, and she's so two-faced, and I'm trying to stop doing those things too but it's hard, it's like I've been trained into that, I don't know.' Rhiannon felt like he was speaking the unspeakable, dredging up a shame from her that ran so deep it was maybe part of her marrow. She slowly began to respond, to nod, to give noises of affirmation or agreement. Thought of how conflicted she was that the thing she loved most in the world, to read, was something she had been gifted by her mum. Thought of the lisp that she had picked up from her in learning to speak, and wondered what else she'd learned from her without even realising. Would she grow up to have a daughter, and be threatened by her daughter as her mum had been by her, and her mum before that, and probably her mum before that? Was it preordained, written into her DNA? Is this why she hated herself so, did she want to kill her mum within her, just as Angela sought to kill her mum within Rhiannon? Soon Rhiannon and Cam moved onto other subjects, but their bond had been cemented. They realised they both loved and had cried over Cyndi Lauper's 'I Want a Mom That Will Last Forever' from *Rugrats in Paris*. Cam had just pulled up YouTube on his phone to play it when Esther came running up, gasping with gales of laughter that shook her whole body.

'Ohhhh my god, guys, the FUNNIEST thing just happened in French, what the fuck.' As usual she launched straight into her story, not bothering to check whether she was interrupting something. 'So the teacher, this woman Maria, her shirt was open and she wasn't wearing a bra and her right breast was showing for, like, ages, and none of us wanted to say anything. And then finally this guy Isaac, you know the hot Islander one, he put up his hand and he was like, 'Excuse me, your aioli is showing,' and she was just confused, because obviously he meant areola but mixed up the word, but by that point we were pissing ourselves so much no one could explain what he actually meant and so –' Esther's breathlessness overtook her and she lay her head on the table and cackled to high heaven. It echoed around the quad and university students looked down from the steps of the library, possibly thinking how silly or how young or how obnoxious she was but really, beneath that, envying her for the mirth that overcame any self-consciousness, as her skirt had ridden up around her hips and she was flashing her g-string to the world, and she didn't notice or care.

Rhiannon went back to Vee's house after school, and the two of them sat with Isla, who now reminisced openly about Orkney, without Vee reining her in. Rhiannon watched her webbed fingers spread upon the glass of whisky she held, tried to imagine them clawed and furred instead. She looked at her singed ear and thought of the ear holes that were under the cheek feathers of Sasha's cockatiels, how you could scritch them and look underneath, to that tiny cavern that pierced their skull. Would Isla's ears be the same as that if she changed? Just a gully for sound to run into, straight into her brain?

Isla's speech grew more incoherent as she refilled her glass, and began to talk about her attempts to find her skin, all well in the past. From what Rhiannon could gather it had been a good ten years since she had tried searching, had resigned herself to her fate after years of disappointment. Looking at her, Rhiannon wondered if she would even be able to make it anywhere if they did find her sealskin – would it just be assisted suicide, letting her swim out into an unknown ocean, far from the one she knew? Surely Vee must see how dangerous, how very absurd, it all was. Some of this was answered for her when Ellie called Rhiannon's mobile, and she picked up to find her tangling her words in agitation.

'Wait, wait, slow down. What are you saying?'

'Sasha. My mum. She has a booking with him. In a month, the second Thursday of the school holidays. She said she'll be able to get any info we need from him then. And that she'll be able to hold him for a few hours also if we need.'

'Hold him – what do you mean hold him?'

Vee snatched the phone from her, 'Ellie, it's Vee... yep... okay... amazing... can you thank her for me.'

'What does she mean "hold him"?' Rhiannon demanded when Vee hung up. 'Well, she's gotta keep him away so we have time to get it if it's hidden somewhere, and time for my mum to escape. We're only going to get this one chance. Speaking of, that's enough for you tonight,' and she took the glass from her mother's hand, something Rhiannon had never seen her do before. 'We're going to have to start weaning you off if you're going to be sober enough to swim in four weeks' time, Mither.'

Isla looked up at her, eyes black and startled. Rhiannon watched as comprehension dashed across the orbs like the swell over a cliff face, washing away the grit and leaving joy in its place.

18

Rhiannon hardly saw Vee over the next month, as she wanted to spend as much time with her mother as possible, just in case they did find her sealskin and it led to her departure. They were tense weeks for Rhiannon, at home with Angela without Vee and her getaway car, and so she spent long days at Ellie's, appearing at any hour, shoes dusty from the six-kilometre walk. As she walked she often cried, a release she was unaccustomed to, usually only brought to her through cutting. Ferns lined the roadside and blurred into a smudge of green against other greens, as she listened to country music on her iPod and thought of the offer Sasha had given her to move in permanently with them if she wanted. It was something she had accepted she needed to do, though her heart ached at the thought of leaving her home, being exiled from it. No longer reading in the boughs of the jacaranda overhanging the road, no longer running barefoot up the curve of the hill, the grass of the lawn damp beneath her soles, no longer watching the day pass across McGrath's Hump, the gradual changes in colour and shadows that told the time and season. And what about Ajax and Tall, and the cows and the chooks – would she ever see them again?

She played Kasey Chambers' 'The Captain' solemnly on repeat, and related to how she sang simultaneously of both loss and freedom. She felt she had found the place she was meant to be, this valley within a valley, she'd never pictured herself anywhere else and imagined a future outside of it. She hadn't felt the rush to get to a metropolis that so many of her restless friends did, didn't feel the call of Bali or the Gold Coast, not even for Schoolies. She knew she would be quite content to stay within her valley forever, except now the place she loved had become the place she dreaded, she had been chased out and, like Dolly Parton said in 'Wildflowers,' she would have to learn to bloom elsewhere.

It was a huge reconfiguration to grapple with. Speaking to Vee about it on the home phone one night, while her mum was out at book club, she found that Sasha had offered the same thing to Vee, and Vee was also considering it.

'Why would I stay at home with my mum gone? She is home to me, not that house or the land it sits on. And besides, I'll have betrayed my dad as far as he's concerned which is another reason to go.'

Vee didn't feel any particular attachment to the property she grew up on, unlike Rhiannon. She felt it for the ocean. The ocean for Vee wasn't one singular beach; it was a continuous undulating mass, a living breathing entity, and as long as she could plunge in whenever she wanted, she felt no separation from it.

It was the last Friday of term, the final Friday before their planned reconnaissance and rescue effort, and after Rhiannon hung up she went to shower. Neither she nor Vee had commented on the fact that if they both took up Sasha's offer they would be living together, as a couple, and she wondered as she soaped herself if that was because neither of them wanted to place too much pressure or emphasis on it, for it to lend a gravity to their relationship that maybe it shouldn't. As she rinsed the suds from between her buttocks, she saw something out of the corner of her eye. Through the full-length window, beyond the bursting gardenia bush that supposedly protected their privacy, she saw the figure of a man, holding up a flip-phone camera, obviously filming her. In the darkness she couldn't see his facial features, and he ran off as she leaped out of the shower and reached for a towel. She sprinted through the house to stand, shivering with wet and cold and fear on the front porch, glaring out at the night. In the distance at the rundown silo across the road, she saw a car's lights flash on and then drive away. With the back number plate helpfully lit up, she could read it and she recognised it instantly – it was her neighbour's car. The same neighbour who she had seen masturbating countless times as she fed Tall. How many other nights had he watched her like this, unsuspecting while she showered, hunched in a hoodie in the dark?

That decided things for her. She was being chased from the valley by more than one force. She would move in with Ellie. Her home wasn't a safe haven.

On the Thursday of the planned meeting, Sasha dropped Ellie and Rhiannon at Vee's on her way to Coffs Harbour. She was meeting Paul in a hotel room at the resort, explained she had a scheduled booking with him from 2pm to 4pm, but she had a way of keeping him longer – till 10am the next morning if need be, when she had to check out of the room – and she had a way of making him talk, once Vee asked whatever questions she needed answers to. They were surprised to find Isla sitting outside, upright in the sun, with bright eyes and a quickness they'd never seen in her before. She said she'd only had two drinks the day before, and was ready for whatever the day had in store for her. No one spoke about what would happen if Sasha couldn't get the information needed from Paul, or if the sealskin didn't exist anymore. They were all aware this was a huge and final gamble, with everything resting upon it, and a contingency plan wasn't possible.

Vee showed them her bedroom where she had packed up all her stuff to fit in her car, once her mum had left and before her dad came home. Her hands and voice were shaking with anticipation. At 1:50pm Sasha texted Ellie to say she was about to meet him, and that she would keep them updated. They pulled chairs out into the backyard to sit with Isla, and began to wait.

Thirty kilometres north and in lieu of a smoke, Sasha chewed the edges of her fingers as she waited for her client. Paul had been a reg for years, someone she could say she trusted, as much as you could trust a client – which was to say he showed up on time, paid her, didn't push her boundaries and didn't try to stealth her. They often acted out different fantasies, so it was not odd for her to suggest they try a new BDSM roleplay for this booking.

She accidently tore a cuticle too far and as it began to bleed, she sucked on her finger to try to ease the blood flow before his arrival. She had already set up a chair in the centre of the room, and gathered together the shibari ropes and rubber gag that she had borrowed from a BDSM mistress who had once worked at the brothel with her. Her mind was alive with the repercussions of what she was about to do. She had no moral qualms, and was perfectly willing to believe what Ellie had said – that Isla needed time to escape from her husband and that there was an item of sentimental value that he kept hidden from her and that she needed to retrieve before she could leave. Sasha had worked with enough women, covering bruises with make-up and stashing away cash to keep hidden from violent partners, to know how difficult it was to leave. She was more concerned with what he might try to do in retaliation – but she was betting on the fact that he wouldn't want to expose himself as the client of a sex worker, or whatever evil deeds had occurred in his marriage, to come after her legally, and she didn't think he was the kind to come after her physically. Most likely he would write terrible reviews of her, in which case she'd have to rebrand. She began to think of new names when there was a discreet knock on the door.

'Bella,' he said, and greeted her with a kiss on the cheek. They made small talk as he handed her the cash and went to shower. She checked the seams of her stockings and that her pussy was neat and free of smegma one final time – she was a professional, after all, even if she was intending on holding him hostage, he would still get the service he paid for.

When he finished showering, she directed him to sit down and stay still as she tied him up and put the ball gag on. She hoped her nerves didn't show; she wasn't a domme and was really making it up as she went along, though she supposed the facade of confidence was half of it. She began to stir his cock with her hand, squeezing the half-hard shape while she pinched at his nipples. A groan came from his throat. She spat on his knob and worked away at it for a bit, till it was lathered with his pre-cum. Then she rustled in her bag beside the bed and pulled out nipple clamps and a candle she had brought. Attaching the clamps to his nipples, she lit the candle and, as she waited for the wax to form, began to lazily fiddle with her clit in front of him, an irresistible tease, then turned around and bent over so he could see her properly finger-fuck herself.

'Okay, Paul, we're going to play a game, and I want you to nod if you understand,' she said as she turned back to face him.

He nodded.

'I want something from you, but I'm not going to take your gag off, because you've been a naughty boy and I don't want you to squeal, so we are going to communicate purely through nods. Seeing as I've deprived you of your hands and voice. Do you understand?'

He nodded, and his dick twitched with the blood pulsing through it. 'When I want an answer from you, if it's not a yes or no answer, we are going to spell out the word together. So I am going to say each letter of the alphabet slowly, and you will nod at the right letter, so I can write it out. Do you understand?' He nodded again, and she could tell he was impressed with how elaborate the roleplay was.

'Let's practise. So, how much do you want me to sit on your cock? A –' he nodded and she began the alphabet again, till together they had spelt out A L O T. 'Great, good boy. I can see you're a fast learner. Now, we're going to add someone else into this, just for some extra fun.' She could see the apprehension in his eyes as she reached for her phone and rang Ellie's number, as they had pre-arranged. 'Vee, you ready? Yep, I've got him here. I'm going to pass you to him now. Ask him whatever you want, he can't answer you right now, let's call him *indisposed*, but once you hang up I'll get the answer from him.'

She held the phone to his ear and watched as his features tightened at the sound of his daughter's voice. She couldn't hear what was said but could see on the screen when Vee had hung up and, putting the phone down, she picked up the lit candle. She slowly poured the hot wax across his chest then, setting it down, she reached for the lighter, squatted down between his knees, and held the flame close to his balls, 'Now, you're going to spell out that answer for me.'

She met his eyes and sensed his body go rigid as he realised the combined seriousness of Vee's demand and Sasha's intent.

'This'll go a lot quicker if you're a good boy.'

Half an hour later Ellie's phone buzzed on her lap and she opened the incoming text immediately. 'Okay so, oh my god, he said 'surfboard shed, wetsuits, inside.' Vee, you know what that means right?'

Vee was up and off already though, running across the lawn to the lean-to, where all the surfboards were stacked. Rhiannon and Ellie scrambled after her, but Isla didn't move. They found Vee hurriedly unzipping the first wetsuit she'd found, which was mouldy with age, and reaching her hands inside. They began to help, each pulling one off the hooks.

'This one smells manky,' Ellie commented as she struggled with the zipper, which was jammed.

A few minutes later Rhiannon and Vee had finished checking the others, and they turned to the one in Ellie's arms; 'We'll have to cut it open,' Rhiannon said. 'I'll go get a knife.'

'Don't worry, there's a Stanley knife here,' Vee said, brandishing it. 'You guys hold it out while I cut it, we'll need to be careful.'

As she began to slice the suit a stench filled the room and Rhiannon muttered 'fuck that's festy' under her breath, not wanting to say it louder in case she insulted Vee, though Vee too had her nose and mouth screwed up. As she pulled back the chest and sleeves she exposed a grey-brown pelt to the air. It slithered out onto the floor. If the girls had expected something mystical they were sorely disappointed. It was missing fur in parts where moths or rodents had gotten to it, and it had a clammy feel from being stored inside the wetsuit. There were freakish eye holes where the head would supposedly go that chilled them all. But Vee leant down and picked it up with care, cradled it tenderly in her arms and carried it outside.

In the sun it looked slightly better, there was a sheen to the sealskin that hadn't been noticeable in the murk. Vee took it across to Isla and then fell to her knees before her, holding it out as if it were a ceremonial offering. Isla reached her hand out, then hesitated, hovering it above while the others held their breath. Then, finally, she stroked it. At first tentatively, then firmly and with unconscious portentousness. The way she handled the sealskin, with both care and awe, transformed it from what had been, to them, an item of other-worldly spookiness and ick, to an object of value. Here was something that was beyond the symbolic, and beyond their comprehension.

As dusk fell Rhiannon and Ellie stood at Third Headland, with the winter wind whistling in their ears forcing them to pull their jacket collars up around their necks. The beach was empty, except for the distant figures of Isla and Vee, standing on some rocks semi-immersed in the surf. As they watched, Isla stepped out of her clothes, and they could see the sag and suffering of her disregarded body, the body that she had hated so much and been condemned to live within for so long. They saw Vee hand the pelt to her, and she seemed to step inside it, as they did into their school skirts. Then, they could only make out a shape on the rocks, a shape that began to undulate and propel itself towards the water's edge, galumphing across the craggy surface. They wondered if it was rough on its stomach, or was any jag a jab of joy after so long away? It slithered into the waves, then seemed to turn back and rest its head on the edge as Vee bent down beside it. They could just make out her hand at its whiskered nose, and for long minutes they stayed like that, till suddenly it sank beneath the waves and Vee was left, standing alone.

'Should we join her?' Ellie asked.

As they moved closer they could hear Vee's sobs, and see that she was crying into her webbed fingers, hands already wet from sea spray and seal slick. They stood with her till the night was dark around them.

Eventually, Vee said, 'Let's go. I need to pack my things. Ellie, you can tell Sasha she can let him go in an hour.' She began to walk back to the car.

19

Five weeks had passed. It was the beginning of September and the sun had lost its sharp winter edge and had somehow become smudged as the air softened with increasing humidity. Rhiannon walked up the hill to the top of her old road, appreciating the optical illusion that made McGrath's Hump appear further away the closer you walked to it, as the trees along the roadside disappeared into your peripheries and the mountain seemed to be solitary against the huge expanse of sky, as if it were the focal point of a landscape painting. She wanted to continue down that curving road, past the pink, peeling gumtree, down into the valley, hoped that Ajax would come running up to greet her, would jump on her and lick her hands. Instead though, she turned back, not wanting to accidentally run into her mum knowing it would soon be time to leave for school. She'd have to pat Fanchette instead, who gloried in the inevitable attention brought by two extra housemates.

She could feel the advent of spring in the air around her, had felt it for days now. Vee drove with the windows down on their trip into school each morning, cruising through Bellingen to pick up Nat on the way. There had been no retaliation from either of their parents when the two girls had relocated to Sasha's. Vee, not wanting to go through the rigamarole of Centrelink forms with her newly estranged father, had picked up a cash-in-hand job at a cafe in town so she could help Sasha with expenses. Rhiannon passed on half of her youth allowance to Sasha, to cover the cost of her living and eating there. Still though, Sasha had to pick up extra shifts to support the new additions, not that she told the girls that, she didn't want them to feel that they were a burden or be conflicted about living off her unholy earnings.

'I'm so jealous you guys get to have a sleepover every night!' Esther exclaimed, as they all sat in the quad at lunch time. A number of their friends were envious about the non-traditional family structure, without considering the dysfunction that had led to its existence; though in

Esther's case she guessed it and chose to ease any discomfort Vee or Rhiannon might be feeling by pretending that it was all in fun.

'You must like miss your home a bit though, hey?' Zoe asked.

'I mean, I do... but I'm still so close to it,' Rhiannon answered, and looked at Vee in the hope she would step in, which she did.

'I don't miss mine at all really, except I do miss being so close to the beach.'

Maybe that was true, but Rhiannon knew Vee missed something else beyond that. She had caught her pouring over a map of Orkney on her laptop a few days earlier, stroking the outline of the Bay of Birsay with the cursor, the tenderness of the lingering touch of the on-screen hand contrasted by the distance of the digital medium. Tens of thousands of kilometres away, schools of seals swam through the waters and gathered in colonies on the shore, their bodies bumping up against each other and shoving each other off crowded shelves of rock. Did they have room for one more in their midst? Would they welcome a lone seal back? Would she even make it that far, or was her long jawed skull resting on an ocean bed, or lying sun bleached in a pebbled cove, her soul free of all restraints?

'We need to make sure she doesn't dwell on it, and lose herself in it,' Ellie said to Rhiannon that night as they sat on the wooden fence posts listening to the horses enjoy their meals, the evening folding them into its subtle embrace.

'What can we do?'

'You know we still haven't really done anything fun to celebrate you being here, or anything to mark your leaving. We were so caught up in the chaos of Sasha holding Paul hostage and Isla finally being free that you guys both just came here, with no hubbub. I mean besides you having to tell your mum you were moving out, of course.'

'Yeah that was heinous. Personally, I think I've had a dramatic enough start to a new chapter. But maybe you're right, maybe we need to do something ritualistic to acknowledge and say goodbye to the old.'

Rhiannon thought of how Vee had spoken of having some sort of memento and asked, 'Do you reckon she would wanna get a tattoo? We could all go together.'

'What and get a naff seal or something? Na fuck that... wait I know what we should do! We should steal the sign.'

'What sign?!'

'The Hungry 4 Head sign! The one on the Pacific Highway turn off. Vee loves it and we could hang it up here and besides it'll be such a fun adventure.'

'We'll have to go at like 3 in the morning... there's too many trucks on the Pacific Highway on a Friday night, we'll get caught before then. Let's ask her now,' and Ellie pushed herself off the post, landing on all fours, cat-like in the dusk.

Rhiannon didn't follow her immediately though, preferring instead to savour the twilight around her and the thoughts that inevitably came on with the twixt of night and day. Something about the changing light that marked the passage of time always conjured up the most emotionally charged phantasmagoria. The sweet scent of slashed paddocks, sheafs of paspalum warmed and dried by the heat of the sun, wafted against her and her mind wandered back to a month before, to the final confrontation with her mum. If she thought she would gain some consolation or closure from the interaction, she was wrong. She was left with no further insight into why her mum treated her the way she did. Perhaps there was something deeply wrong with her, like her mother said, and that's what spurred Angela's cruelty. Perhaps even Angela didn't know what drove her to say the things she said or do the things she did. Perhaps it would take Rhiannon her whole life to understand, or perhaps it would always be incomprehensible to her, an impenetrable mystery with none of the allure of the complicated characters of the books she so loved.

She had told her she was moving out, and it had gone exactly as she expected. Allegations of her being ungrateful, of deserting her after she had 'given her so much,' of her leaving being a reflection of her disregard for and inability to form emotional attachments. Rhiannon had held herself back, as she always did, till finally there was a pause and into that pause she spat.

'How could you have told people that?'

'What?'

'You know – *that*. That I was sleeping with my dad. Or that he was abusing me, whatever.'

'*I* didn't tell people that, they suggested it to me. And I just asked people whether or not they thought it was true. I was doing my duty as a mother.'

'So you spread it. Instead of asking me?' Rhiannon's hands shook as she spoke, both terrified and thrilled by the fact she was standing up for herself for once.

'I did ask you, and you didn't answer. Which made it very likely to be true – I mean, I wouldn't put it past him – '

'You didn't ask me. You just told me that it was one of the things wrong with me, in amongst all the other things wrong with me. You spoke to me exactly the way you complain that grandma speaks to you.'

For one brief moment it had seemed as if her mum might take on and contemplate something she had said, but force of habit was too strong and she bit back with her usual defence.

'Don't put the blame on me! It's not *my* fault that you are the way you are, do you think I wanted a daughter like you, one who can't even cry or feel? Look at you now, not even reacting and we're talking about what's been done to you to make you this way, a normal girl would be…' her voice had followed Rhiannon as she walked out of the house, across the lawn and turned to walk up the road. She walked out with nothing, having moved most of her clothes with Ellie a few days before, unbeknownst to Angela. She had walked up Little North Arm Road and as she walked she had begun to sob, a sob that she had covered with a brittle smile and wave when a neighbour drove past her. She had walked herself out of that constant pretence and straight to Ellie's, Ellie's that was now her refuge. Ellie's that had all the sounds and smells of home but wasn't quite it. Maybe she did need something to bookend the transition as much as Vee did.

'Nat, can you shine the torch more on the bolts,' Vee said, tottering at the top of a step ladder, with a crescent wrench in her hand.

'Sorry, I got distracted looking to see if there were any cars coming.'

'That's my job,' Ellie said, from where she stood with both hands stabilising the base of the ladder, 'I can hold the ladder and look out.'

'How many girls does it take to unscrew a road sign?' Rhiannon said and they all cackled.

'Don't make me laugh, these bolts are so tight as it is and the wrench keeps slipping off,' Vee protested. 'You're going to need to pass me the vice-grip. It should be in the boot.'

'Is there really going to be enough room in here for us to fit the sign?' Rhiannon asked as she rustled around in it.

'Of course, are you kidding, it's a Commodore. Plenty of space,' Vee defended her car.

She thanked Rhiannon as she passed her the vice-grip, and began to unscrew the bolts as quickly as she could. They were all jittery with excitement and nerves, laughing at each other's amateur fumbling.

'Ow, Nat, you just whacked me with the torch,' Ellie said, through a fit of giggles.

'Sorry I'm really bad at this, I'm not made for – oh my god a car's coming! Everyone duck down!'

'I can't fucking duck down I'm on the ladder, and I don't wanna jump in the dark,' Vee protested angrily.

'Then just stay still behind the sign, I can see its headlights now.

It's coming from Coffs direction, which is good,' Nat said softly, from where she lay flat on the ground.

'Don't you lay down, Ellie! I need you to hold the ladder still or I'll fall!' Ellie, chastened, hurriedly kneeled behind the ladder and put her hands back on the rungs. As she did so the car careened around the corner, its lights momentarily illuminating them. If the driver was paying attention they would've seen both the legs of the ladder and a person protruding from beneath the road sign. Rhiannon and Nat were well hidden in the long grass of the verge, stalks tickling their nostrils as they tried to turn their hysterical squeals into quiet breaths.

'Okay they're gone. I've only got one bolt left – Nat, light me up!'

'Action!' Rhiannon cried as she leapt back up.

Three minutes later they were wrangling the sign into the boot, and folding the step ladder up to lie on top of it.

'What a good car,' Ellie said, patting its rump proudly.

'And what a good team, I have to say. We've done a good day's work,' Rhiannon congratulated them all as she slammed the boot shut. 'Now you've got a piece of your old home for your new home, Vee.'

'And I'll treasure it forever. I'll treasure you guys forever, too. Now, let's get out of here,' and she rammed her foot on the accelerator so that the tires skidded on the gravel as they took off.

'Gun it!' Ellie yelled delightedly.

They took the back roads back to Gleniffer, dropping Nat off in Bellingen on the way, concerned about being pulled over on Waterfall Way and a cop seeing their stash in the back. When they got to Ellie's they found Sasha sitting on the porch, glowing ember visible between her fingers.

'Sorry, did we wake you?' Ellie asked apologetically as they walked towards her. 'No, don't worry. I couldn't sleep. So thought I'd try a joint. Did you want some?'

Rhiannon took it from her outstretched hand, and then gushed excitedly, 'We've just been stealing the Hungry 4 Head road sign! Do you want to see it?' Sasha laughed and laughed, till they all joined in and couldn't stop, each time one eased they got carried along in the flow of another. Finally, she stopped with her hand held to her chest, as if trying to hold the laughter in to prevent it from bursting out. 'God, my cheeks are aching. I'm alright thanks, girls, I'll have a look in the morning.'

Ellie sat down on the ground and leaned against her mother's legs, while Vee took the spare seat and pulled Rhiannon onto her lap. They all smoked the rest of the joint in silence, listening to the spring sound of the crickets, returning for another year, another short life of mating and song. The first beetles of the summer thronged around the bare bulb above them, competing with moths for that electric halo, as tantalising as the moon, an occasional zap as one burned its wings and toppled to the ground, Icarus's folly in miniature.

'Have you spoken to your mum, Vee? How's she going?' Sasha asked, and Rhiannon stiffened out of anticipation and protectiveness.

Vee squeezed her waist in reassurance and said, 'I think she's going to be okay.'